First Meeting

"You creep!" he cried. "How could you do it?" His voice was vehement, full of fury, and the spit flew out of his mouth from the force of his words.

I moved back from my window at first, terrified at this nutty kid snarling at me. Anger overcame me. Anger at the loss of my own precious fire escape.

"What are you doing on my side of the fire escape anyway? This side belongs to me."

"I hate it here," the boy yelled. "I hate you and I hate what you're doing—you, you murderer!"

Other Avon Flare Books by
Marilyn Sachs

BABY SISTER
CLASS PICTURES

Fourteen

BY MARILYN SACHS

AN AVON FLARE BOOK

AVON BOOKS
A division of
The Hearst Corporation
105 Madison Avenue
New York, New York 10016

Book design by Claire Counihan
Avon cover photograph by Abe Rezny
Published by arrangement with E.P. Dutton
Library of Congress Catalog Card Number: 82-18209
ISBN: 0-380-69842-0

The E.P. Dutton edition contains the following Library of Congress Cataloging in Publication Data

Sachs, Marilyn.
Fourteen.
Summary: Having to contend with a suffering poet-father and an author-mother who uses her daughter's life as material for her popular books, fourteen-year-old Rebecca finds her life is further disrupted by the new boy next door and his enigmatic family.
[1. Mothers and daughters—Fiction. 2. Friendship—Fiction]
I. Title.
PZ7.S1187Fo 1983 [Fic.] 82-18209

First Avon Flare Printing: January, 1985

Printed in the U.S.A.

K-R 20 19 18 17 16

for Jessica Meyers,
who graduated with honors from being fourteen

Fourteen

Chapter 1

My mother has just finished writing a new book. This one is a teenage romance, and when she first started it, I was miserable. Because even though she tried her best, she never could manage to keep me out of her stories.

She has written fourteen books now, one for each year of my life. They've all been about me in one horrible way or another, and I hated them all. But I didn't know I hated them until I was six and my mother's fifth book, *Rebecca Goes to School*, came out. By then I had a girlfriend named Karen Blue, who had known me since kindergarten and who hurried to point out some interesting differences between the Rebecca in the book and me.

"She's prettier than you were in kindergarten, Rebecca, and her clothes fit her better. You always wore wrinkled tee shirts and you never had all the friends she has. And your nose used to run all the time and Ms. Jamison had to tell you to wipe it."

I had my first temper tantrum when I got home from Karen's house that day. I fell down on the ground, kicked my feet up and down and screamed as loud as I could. When I finished, there were tears in my mother's eyes. She held me in her arms, kissed me and apologized over and over again for violating my privacy.

"Never, never again," she promised. "I'll never do it again."

But the next book, she did it again.

"How can you accuse me of such a thing?" cried my mother. "I didn't call the main character Rebecca. Her name is Nancy, and she has three sisters . . ."

"And lots of freckles," I yelled, "especially in the summertime. And she has blue eyes . . ."

"Lots of people have blue eyes and freckles," said my mother.

"But they don't have trouble pronouncing their *R*s."

"Nobody would know it was you, darling," said my mother earnestly. "After all, think of all the things that happen to Nancy. She has to have her tonsils out, and you've never even been to a hospital. And her father buys her a beautiful dollhouse . . ."

"Just like the one I wanted for my birthday when I was five," I said bitterly.

"But you know, darling, it was very, very expensive, and we just couldn't afford it. And besides, Daddy made you one, didn't he? Nobody ever had a dollhouse like yours."

Which was true. My father takes great pride in his woodworking skills, and the dollhouse that he made me still stands, or I should say wobbles, on the floor in my room. It looks nothing like the magnificent one Nancy's father gives her in my mother's book. Every year I think, now I can put it away. Now that I'm twelve or thirteen or fourteen, Dad will understand that I'm too old for it and he won't be hurt. But because it embarrasses me so much and always did, and because he thinks of it as his crowning achievement, and because I love him too much to hurt his feelings, I suppose I'll never get rid of it. I suppose it will go with me when I leave home, when I marry, when I have children. And probably when I die somebody will say, "She loved that dollhouse so much it should be buried with her."

But I was talking about my mother and her Rebecca books. Because all of them are Rebecca books. Even though the main characters are now called Nancy or Maryanne or Yoriko or Sally Jean, all of them are me but with a twist.

"See," said my mother proudly about her twelfth book, "the main character is called Maryanne, and she has long, black hair and dark eyes, and she's short and a little on the heavy side . . ."

"And she throws up all over her mother's shoe, the way I did when I had stomach flu."

"Ah," said my mother triumphantly, "but Maryanne has leukemia and is throwing up because she's nauseous from the chemotherapy."

"Is she going to live?" I asked my mother nervously. "You kind of leave it up in the air at the end of the book."

"I think so," said my mother, "but you have to stop thinking that those characters are you. I purposely made Maryanne the exact opposite of you in every way."

It's like the dark side of the moon.

My friends think I'm lucky. They beg me to use my influence with my mother so that they can show up in her books, too. They don't understand how humiliating it is to see a twisted version of yourself in every book she writes.

"How can you say such a thing?" said my mother. "Look at Yoriko." She was talking about her thirteenth book. "First of all, she's half Japanese."

"So I'm half Jewish."

"It's not the same thing at all. And then she has a crush on an absolutely worthless boy."

I immediately burst into tears.

"Now Rebecca, why in the world are you crying about that?"

"Because you know very well that I had a crush on Peter Johnson."

"But Rebecca, Peter is the best-looking kid in the school and the nicest. I purposely had Yoriko fall for a mean, selfish boy with a broken nose who steals money from his mother's purse. Peter never would do anything like that."

"And he never tried to make out with me either."

"Well, there you are. Yoriko has to really fight him off in that chapter down in the cafeteria."

"That's what I mean. At least she gets to fight him off. You always let them do things I never do. But you get all your ideas from me. And you keep listening to me and watching me. It's like I'm being tracked all the time."

My mother's lips began trembling. "I try so hard," she said. "Each time I think I'm finally going to write something that Rebecca will like."

"I do like them," I sobbed. "I love them. If you weren't my mother, you'd be my favorite author. But the girls in your stories are always me or the exact opposite of me or nearly me or twice as much as me, but they all have such interesting things happen to them."

"But so do you," wept my mother. "You have interesting things happen to you too."

"Like what?" I cried.

By this time the two of us were drowning in tears, so we had to concentrate on cheering each other up. We hugged and kissed, and I said I knew she didn't really mean to hurt my feelings, and she promised to try harder next time not to put me into her story.

"Why don't you do another one about Arthur?" I suggested, trying to point her in the direction of my kid brother.

My mother looked terrified. She tried to do one a few years ago about a boy who plays Little League softball, as Arthur does. She trooped off with him every afternoon he played but she never seemed to be able to understand the game.

"I tried," she said. "You remember, Rebecca, but it was such a boring story nobody wanted to buy it. And besides, it's hard for me to understand boys. Arthur was very patient and answered all my questions, but I never could get into how he thinks."

"Maybe because he doesn't think at all."

My mother brightened and said, "But this time, for sure, I'm going to do a book that won't have anything to do with you."

I looked doubtful.

"I'm going to do a real romance," said my mother.

"Thanks a lot," I told her. "I thought the one about Yoriko was a romance."

"No," she said, "because nothing really happens, and Yoriko gets over it and goes on to become a potential ballet star."

"Thanks for that too," I said, remembering my disastrous ballet lessons when I was ten and eleven. Nobody ever for a moment thought of me as a potential ballet star.

"No, my new book will be about a girl called—Okay, Rebecca, you tell me. You pick a name this time. Any name you like."

"How about Melanie? That doesn't sound anything like Rebecca."

"Fine. I'll call her Melanie."

My mother beamed at me, but I remained unconvinced. "Well, what's going to happen to her?"

"Oh, I guess she'll fall in love with a real nice boy, and he'll fall in love with her. See, Rebecca, you can't say anything like that ever happened to you."

I couldn't argue with her. Because up to then she was absolutely right. No boy had ever tried to kiss me in the school cafeteria or anyplace else. I'd had plenty of one-sided crushes, like electric shocks, ever since sixth grade when Jonas Frampton accidentally sat on my lunch. But as far as I knew, they had never been returned.

"Maybe I'll call it *First Love*," said my mother, "and the girl will be—fifteen, I think. Fourteen is too young, at least in a book. Publishers like the girl to be fifteen or sixteen. Maybe I'll make the boy a year or two older. They have to be older in books. But she—Melanie—will be pretty and smart. No, I better not make her smart. You'll get upset if she's smart."

"I'll get upset if she's dumb too, because then I'll know you're trying to make her the opposite of me. You can make her kind of smart—like a B+ student."

"Okay," said my mother, "and I'll make her a sophomore. See Rebecca, you're only a freshman. And the boy will be a senior. Maybe he'll be president of the student council and she can be a delegate and—there has to be some kind of conflict or problem. Maybe she'll think he's too bossy or maybe he should think she's too bossy—but at the end, they'll fall in love and maybe he'll take her to his prom." My mother's eyes shone. "This time, Rebecca, you won't have to worry at all. She won't be anything like you."

That was how my mother began her fourteenth book, *First Love*. I have to admit that I was suspicious, but as it turned out she was right. Her story isn't anything at all like mine.

Chapter 2

My mother doesn't cook much during the week. On Wednesdays, we all usually go out for pizza, and on the other weekdays, my father generally does the cooking. It may not be great, but it certainly is creative. And we can always look forward to one of my grandmother's cakes for dessert.

During the week, my father kids around a lot and makes up funny limericks about us.

There once was a girl named Rebecca
Who buttered both sides of her crecker
Her mother was shocked
Her father, he mocked
And she told them to all go to Mecca.

or

There once was a boy named Arthur
Who thought that baths were a bother
Each night he would yell
"If you don't like my smell,
Try moving a little bit farther."

My mother never dresses up during the week. She wears jeans and turtlenecks or old faded Indian blouses. But on weekends, everything changes. My mother does the cooking, and we eat things like quiches and bouillabaisses and hot Indian curries. And she puts on a pair of slacks or even a dress and tries to have the house tidied up before my poor father comes home. Because on weekends, my father is always depressed.

During the week, Arthur and I get up before seven o'clock, eat breakfast, and go off to school. My parents don't usually get up much before nine on weekdays and seldom get to bed before one or two in the morning. Both of them are writers and both work at home. Our apartment isn't very large, so Mom generally writes in their bedroom while Dad takes over the kitchen. My father doesn't write children's books the way my mother does. He's a poet. He looks like a poet too, with dark, wavy hair, a high forehead and deep, suffering eyes. They're not suffering during the week when he's writing poems at the kitchen table and cooking our dinners. But on the weekends, when he goes to work in Grandpa's pharmacy, then his eyes are the true, tragic eyes of the genuine poet.

Mom tries but seldom manages to get up and have breakfast with him on Saturday and Sunday mornings. But Arthur always gets up early, and sometimes I do too. Arthur believes in hearty breakfasts because his coach says it's important for athletes to start the day right, so he usually serves my father a big bowl of hot oatmeal with sliced bananas and raisins. Most of the time, my father doesn't eat the oatmeal. He just drinks a cup of coffee and suffers.

"It's not so bad," I tell him, in the special soft, cooing voice the three of us use on him weekends. "It will be over in another day."

"Another day!" he moans. "I don't know if I can get through."

"Eat your oatmeal," Arthur urges. "It will give you a lot of strength."

"There was an accident on the bridge today," my father says morosely. "Three people were killed."

"Well, you're not going over the bridge, so you don't have to worry," I tell him.

"And yesterday, a bomb went off in the Egyptian consulate."

My father never listens to the news during the week. It's only on weekends when the clock radio wakes him up in the morning that he hears the news. He always takes it hard.

"What was the weather?"

"Fair and sunny."

"Great," says Arthur cheerfully. "I'm playing softball in Golden Gate Park today. I was afraid it might rain."

"They always say fair and sunny," says my father mournfully.

"Because it usually is fair and sunny," I tell him.

Somehow or other my father manages to get dressed and take off. When he comes home, my mother has soft music playing and pours him a big, cold glass of white wine as soon as he staggers through the door. Her eyes are always filled with pity, and she never fights with him on Saturdays or Sundays.

"If only I could sell one of my stories to the movies or TV," she says, "your poor father wouldn't have to go to work."

"But he worked as a pharmacist for years before he became a poet," I say. "Didn't he ever like it?"

"No," she says fiercely, "he never liked it. He always suffered. I knew it, and I told him after we were married that life was too short to spend it doing something you hated. I urged him to be true to himself. If it weren't for me, he'd still be working full time as a pharmacist in his father's store."

My grandmother agrees. "If it weren't for her," says my grandmother, "he'd still be working full time in your grandfather's store."

"But Mom says he was unhappy. Mom says he hated it."

"No, no, no," says my grandmother. "He loved it, and the customers were crazy about him. Grandpa was so proud. They were going to be partners, and then Grandpa would be able to retire early and your father would have the store himself until maybe Arthur grew up."

"Arthur doesn't want to be a pharmacist. Arthur wants to be a pitcher."

"Arthur is only a baby."

"But I want to be a pharmacist, Grandma."

My grandmother sighs. "Your grandpa is sixty-two years old. He could retire if your father would only come to his senses and take over the store. He'll never make a living as a poet. Especially with the kind of poems he writes."

"I'm fourteen, Grandma. In ten years, I can be a pharmacist and Grandpa can retire."

"He should only live so long."

I love my grandfather's store. The trouble is it's in Daly City, so I can't get to it unless one of my parents drives me there. It's a beautiful store, full of beautiful-sounding things—Dulcolax, Ben-Gay, lanolin, Vaseline. . . . My father says no, but I wonder if he didn't become a poet because he was surrounded by so many poetic words. You can murmur them over and over again to yourself—Mum, Lavoris, Excedrin. . . . I love the sound of them and the feel of the different tubes and bottles and boxes. You can walk up and down the aisles and marvel at all the brilliant colors and shapes waiting for you to select them. At the cosmetic counter, the samples of the perfumes make the air more fragrant than any florist's—Guerlain, Givenchy, Ma Griffe. . . . And the names of the lipsticks and nail polishes sometimes make me want to weep—Rambling Rose, Flaming Brandy, Passion Flower. . . .

I know where everything is, and sometimes my grandfather lets me arrange the stock. He is a tall, distinguished-looking man who always wears a white coat and listens intently to his customers' problems.

"Doc," they call him. "What do you think I should use for sunburn? . . . For acid indigestion? . . . For athlete's foot? . . . For hemorrhoids? . . . Doc, I got something in my eye. . . . Doc, what can I do for my arthritis?"

My grandfather calls himself the "Poor Man's Doctor." He loves his work, and I know when I become a pharmacist I'll love it too. My grandfather is very proud of me. He says my first sentence was "Gimme more Desitin," which shows I have a bent towards pharmacy. If I lived closer, he would let me work in his store every day after school. Now that I'm fourteen, I tell him, I can start coming in on weekends with Dad. He says Christmas will be a good time to start.

"Just promise you won't retire, Grandpa, until I can take over the store."

"I'm never going to retire," says my grandfather. "Why should I retire? I love my work."

"Grandma wants you to retire. Grandma says if

Daddy had stayed a full-time pharmacist, you'd be able to retire."

"Don't worry," says my grandfather. "I'll wait for you. We'll be partners. Cooper and Cooper," he says, "grandfather and granddaughter."

My mother doesn't approve of my career choice.

"You could be a writer," she says. "You always had a flair for words."

My mother thinks nothing is better than writing. Or, if you can't be a writer, the next best thing would be a painter or some other kind of artist.

"You did some very nice pastel drawings in the art class you took over at the De Young Museum, and you used to make some very interesting collages in school. I remember a spectacular one you did using drug labels and aspirin bottle caps. . . ." She stops herself, but it's too late.

"You see," I tell her, "I like handling drugs. I like medicines. I want to be a pharmacist."

"You're young," she says. "Maybe you'll change your mind."

"No," I tell her. "I won't change my mind. Two writers in the family are enough. I want to be a pharmacist and go into business with Grandpa. I always wanted to be a pharmacist. And besides, I certainly don't want any child of mine to go through what I've had to go through."

"You could write for adults," my mother says, "or you could write nonfiction—maybe books about travel or whales or astronomy."

"Maybe I could," I say, "but I won't because I want to be a pharmacist."

My mother doesn't nag me. Even when she doesn't approve, she never nags. Neither does my father.

When I was younger, I used to long for the kind of attention other girls' parents lavished on them. Karen Blue's mother always gets up early to cook Karen and her sisters a hot breakfast. While it's true that Arthur has been cooking me hot breakfasts for the past few years, it isn't really the same. And my mother never notices if my clothes are creased or my shoes are down at the heels. Other girls' fathers pick them up and drive them places. My father hardly ever drives anywhere except to my grandfather's store. And nobody notices if Arthur or I take showers or when we change the sheets on our beds.

The funny thing is that Mom and Dad are home much more than most kids' parents. They're usually there when we come home from school, and many days, especially when we were younger, they would take us biking in the park or hunting for sand dollars down at Ocean Beach. Even though they have more free time than most parents, they spend very little of it on domestic matters.

"*I* always bake when *I* have spare time," says my grandmother. Once a week, she comes over, bringing a cake or cookies to put into our freezer. She averts her eyes from all the moldy leftovers in the refrigerator and the grimy crust that lines its walls.

My grandmother likes to have Arthur and me spend time alone over at her house. She lives in Daly City in a neat house with a palm tree on her front lawn. Everybody on her street has a palm tree on the front lawn. My father grew up in that house along with his brother, Leonard, who is an accountant and lives in Tucson, Arizona. Everything gleams in my grandmother's house. There is a chandelier with hundreds of tiny, teardrop crystals that hangs over her dining room table, and twice a year my grandmother washes each tiny teardrop with ammoniated water.

When I come to stay over, I sleep in my father's old bed. My grandmother irons the sheets I sleep on and gets up in the mornings to make me waffles with maple syrup. Sometimes she takes me shopping for new clothes and often she brings my shoes in to the shoemaker for heels. I like to talk to my grandmother. I tell her all sorts of things, confidential things, things I never tell my mother because I know my grandmother will never put them into a book. My grandmother is interested in everything I have to tell her. She is particularly interested in my other grandmother, my mother's mother. Grandma and Grandpa Harper live in Cedar Rapids, Iowa, in a white house with a big garden around it without a palm tree. Arthur and I used to spend our summers there, and Grandma Cooper is always interested in hearing what Grandma Harper has to say.

"She says the same thing you do, Grandma. She says Daddy should have stayed a pharmacist. She agrees with you, Grandma."

My grandmother waits. She knows more is coming.

"She says Mom never should have let him quit working in the pharmacy."

My grandmother snorts.

"She says it's not right that Mom should make all the money and Daddy should be home, writing bad poems and doing nothing."

"Who made him?" cries my grandmother. "He was a decent, hard-working man until she came along. She had a sty, and he told her to bathe it in boric acid. I know all about it. I was there when she came back to thank him, and she stayed talking to him and talking to him and there were customers waiting . . ."

But if my Grandmother Cooper doesn't approve of my mother, she approves of Arthur and me, especially me. My Uncle Leonard in Tucson, Arizona, has two sons, both in college, so I'm the only granddaughter. My grandmother likes to knit sweaters for me, and she likes to watch me eat.

"You're too thin," my grandmother says. "Your mother should see that you eat better. She should make you a good hot breakfast every morning."

"Arthur always makes me a good hot breakfast but, Grandma, I don't want to be fat. Nobody wants to be fat nowadays."

My grandmother smiles slyly. "It's starting already," she says. "There's a boy, I bet."

"There's always a boy," I tell her. "But they're never interested in me."

"Don't be stupid," says my grandmother. "With your beautiful face, they'll be falling at your feet any day now."

So I end up telling her all about Peter Johnson or Jonas Frampton and all the boys in between, and she gives me good advice. How to make a boy feel confident. How to be careful not to let them know how smart you are. How to laugh at their jokes. How to dress in more feminine clothes. How to . . . There are lots of how to's, and at different times, and with different boys, I've tried them all, sometimes in combinations and sometimes alone. None of them ever worked.

Chapter 3

There is something else, besides working in my grandfather's store on weekends, that brings a tragic look to my father's eyes. It is the sight of my report cards whenever I bring them home.

"Well, I can't help it," I tell him.

His dark eyes fill with pain. "It was the same with me," he says. "I was always the first in my class too, all the way through school."

"Maybe you're trying too hard," says my mother. "Maybe you should spread yourself out a little more. The girl in my new book, Melanie, is taking *taekwondo*."

"No thanks," I tell her. "I like studying and I like getting all A's."

"I did too," says my father, shaking his head.

My favorite place to study is out on our fire escape. It's a long one, three stories up above the ground, with a piece of a view down at the end away from the street. Our apartment is towards the front of the building, so we only have views of the street and the alley on the side through our windows. The back apartment, which has a higher rental than ours, has magnificent views over the tops of houses, curving down to the ocean. We share the fire escape with the people who live in the rear apartment. For most of the time that we've lived here, Mr. and Mrs. Henderson and their two boys had the apartment. The Hendersons both worked, and the boys were already in high school when we first moved in. After a while, they went off to college and came home only for holidays and summers.

So I had the fire escape pretty much to myself. I could sit on our side anytime I wanted. But when the Hendersons were away, I could move down all the way to their end and sit there with the city spread out beneath me. The Hendersons always kept their drapes closed when they were gone, so I couldn't see into their apartment. Not that I needed to, because they were both very friendly people and were always inviting us to drop in.

Arthur never likes to study on the fire escape. Arthur never likes to study anywhere. So the fire escape belongs to me. I should say the fire escape belongs to me and the dying plants.

We all like plants in my family. My mother, particularly, has a weakness for Boston ferns. Every few months she buys a new one. When she brings it home, she puts it in her bedroom on her desk, and every morning when she writes, she likes to look deep into its green fronds. But sooner or later, mostly sooner, the fern turns sickly and begins shedding its leaves. Sometimes it happens because my mother forgets to water it, and sometimes it's because she doesn't. But she keeps trying, and as the days pass and the fern grows balder and more shriveled, my mother engages in a life-and-death struggle. She always loses.

But she's too kindhearted to condemn any plant to death by throwing it out before its final gasp. That's where the fire escape comes in.

"Maybe it needs a little fresh air," my mother says. "Maybe it will revive outside."

We all know it won't, but out it goes to join four or five other terminal cases, and my mother is free to buy another young, healthy plant.

Every so often, she will buy an African violet or a rex begonia. It never really matters what she buys—all are doomed to end up eventually on the fire escape until they expire and can be dumped into the garbage can.

I'm used to them. Once in a while, I even remember to water them. But the fire escape is my sanctuary. It is the only place where I know I can be alone. The house next to ours is only two stories and its rooftop is on the same level as my fire escape, so I have complete privacy. All I have to do is open my bedroom window and climb outside. I'm out there just about every day after school except when it rains or is very cold. Sometimes at night, I climb outside and look at the stars. One night I even fell asleep and woke up in the dawn with my arm around an emaciated Boston fern.

The Hendersons moved away in September on one of those mild, golden days. I had brought my American history book out on the fire escape to read about Gettysburg. Everything felt different. I knew they had moved, but it was startling and scary not seeing their drapes hanging in front of their window. The room lay open and exposed. It embarrassed me to look at it through the window—empty of furniture, with all its walls and floors showing like a naked body. It worried me, too, thinking about that empty room. Who would live there next? Maybe somebody who never drew his / her drapes and who also demanded a piece of the fire escape for his / her own use.

Now I smile when I think of it, but then I was fearful. I hoped a middle-aged couple just like the Hendersons would move in. I couldn't bear the idea of sharing my fire escape with a stranger.

"Well," said my mother one afternoon when I returned from school, "our new neighbors have arrived."

My heart began beating high up around my ears. "What kind of people?" I demanded. "How many? How old?"

"I'm not sure how many. I only saw two. I was taking out the garbage, and the moving men were carrying up a piano."

"A piano?" said my father thoughtfully.

"Yes," said my mother. "I think that's a pretty good sign. Somebody must be musical. Maybe it's a girl. Maybe she's even Rebecca's age. Wouldn't that be nice, Rebecca, if there's a girl your age?"

My mother had a hungry smile on her face. I knew what she was really thinking, Wouldn't it be nice if there were a musical girl next door who might serve as raw material for one of my books? My mother wasn't thinking of me. I was thinking of that empty bedroom and my fire escape. No, it wouldn't be at all nice for me if a girl my age moved next door.

"Did you see anybody?" I asked.

"Well, yes—a woman about my age. She was carrying some plants upstairs—I don't think there were any Boston ferns. And I was about to say something to her, but the movers nearly dropped the piano and she said—well, I didn't think it was the right time to introduce myself."

"Did you see anybody else?"

"Only a boy—Arthur should be pleased. I couldn't see exactly how old he was. He was also carrying some plants, but he didn't look very tall. Of course you can never tell with boys."

"I hope they don't play the piano during the day," said my father.

"Probably they won't until the late afternoon. And you never write poetry in the late afternoon. Probably they—the parents I mean—will go to work like most people," said my mother cheerfully, "and the children will go to school."

"Why do you say children?" I demanded.

"Because it's a three-bedroom apartment like ours," said my mother, "so I figure a bedroom for the parents, one for the boy and the other for the girl who plays the piano."

She wasn't thinking of me at all. It infuriated me. "And how do you know the parents will go to work?" I said. "How do you know they're not writers like you or musicians? How do you know they won't stay home and play the piano during the day?"

My parents looked alarmed. Why should I be the only one to worry about our new neighbors? Maybe my parents had something to worry about too.

My mother moved over towards the freezer compartment of the refrigerator. She opened it up and inspected the interior. "There's only one way to find out," she said.

"What will you do if they are musicians?" I pressed

on. "What will you do if one of them plays the violin while the other one plays the piano?"

"I never thought of that," said my father.

"Maybe the children play instruments too," I continued relentlessly. "Maybe one of them plays the trumpet and the other plays the drums."

My father groaned and my mother said, still looking into the freezer, "Sometimes, Rebecca, I think you have a cruel streak. Come over here and help me decide."

"Decide what?"

"What kind of cake we should bring our new neighbors. It's always nice to make new people feel welcome, and we may as well get it over with and find out who they are."

"Don't give them a chocolate cake."

"I don't think we have any chocolate cakes left."

"Is there a prune cake? Give them a prune cake. I hate prune cake."

"What about some of these banana muffins? Your grandmother made three dozen banana muffins, so I think we can spare a dozen or so of those."

"Don't give them the banana muffins," said my father. "I always like to have a banana muffin before I go to bed. It comforts me, especially on weekends. I don't like to run out."

"But we have three dozen."

"Why don't you give them a prune cake?" my father insisted.

So my mother pulled out a prune cake, combed her hair, and the two of us, wearing phony smiles, knocked at the door of our new neighbors' apartment. We could hear moving, sliding sounds from inside, but nobody answered the door.

"Ring the bell," I said to my mother. "I don't think they heard you."

My mother rang the doorbell, and we could hear all the sounds suddenly cease inside. Nobody answered the door.

"I'm sure they heard the bell," my mother whispered, the phony smile still on her face.

"Try once more. Maybe they're hard of hearing."

"Not if they play the piano."

"Remember Beethoven? He played the piano and he was deaf."

My mother rang the bell again. Something dropped and then we heard footsteps.

The door opened and a frowning woman stood there, glaring at us.

"Yes?" she said.

"Well," said my mother brightly, "how do you do, Mrs. . . ."

The woman cocked her head to one side and did not offer to tell us her name.

". . . Uh . . . We are your neighbors next door," my mother continued, her smile beginning to sag around the edges. ". . . Catherine Cooper, and this is my daughter, Rebecca. We wanted to say hello and to bring you a little something." My mother held out my grandmother's prune cake, wrapped in foil.

The woman looked at it suspiciously and shrank back. "What is it?" she said.

"It's a cake," said my mother, her arms still outstretched.

"A prune cake," I explained. "My grandmother made it. She's a wonderful baker and particularly famous for her prune cake."

"I never eat cake," said the woman.

"But your family," my mother said, "maybe your family would like some cake."

"No, no," said the woman. "He doesn't eat cake either."

She slammed the door, leaving my mother still holding the cake, the remains of her smile quickly fading from her face.

"Well?" asked my father when we returned.

"They don't like cake," I told him.

My mother said, "I don't think we'll have to worry too much about them bothering us, Michael. You remember how the Hendersons were always asking us in for drinks, and you used to feel kind of pressured."

"That's good," said my father, "but did you find out if they're musicians?"

"We didn't find out anything except they don't like cake. The woman slammed the door in our faces."

"Oh yes, we did find something out," my mother said. She put the prune cake back in the freezer and turned, grinning at us.

"Well, what did you find out?" I asked. "She slammed that door so fast I could hardly see what she looked like except that she's skinny and mean looking."

"There are only two of them," my mother said triumphantly. "When she said she didn't eat cake, I said, 'Maybe your family would like some.' And she said, 'No, *he* doesn't eat cake either.' So that means there are only two of them. Probably she's a divorced woman with that young boy. She didn't look like a pianist. Probably she has to go to work and the boy will go to school, so . . ."

"Thank God," said my father. "Maybe I'll have a banana muffin right now to celebrate."

I left my parents rejoicing together in the kitchen. But so far I had nothing to celebrate. One kid, even though he was only a young boy like Arthur, could threaten my domain. I hurried into my bedroom, flung open my window and . . .

There was a boy, sobbing out on the fire escape. Not even sobbing on his end, on the scenic side, but over on my end. He was crouched over something just outside my window. His sobs sounded loud and clear, and as he turned towards me I could see that his face was gummy with tears. At that time the only other thing I noticed was that he had very pale, almost white hair that curled around his head.

"You creep!" he cried. "How could you do it?" His voice was vehement, full of fury, and the spit flew out of his mouth from the force of his words.

I moved back from my window at first, terrified at this nutty kid snarling at me. He had something cradled in his arms—a bomb? A knife?

Anger overcame me. Anger at the loss of my own precious fire escape. Before I could stop, I leaped forward and began yelling at him.

"How dare you talk to me like that! And what are you doing on my side of the fire escape anyway? You have no right being here. This side belongs to me."

"I hate it here," the boy yelled. "I hate you and I hate what you're doing—you, you murderer!"

I should have slammed down the window and run for help. Who in her right mind would stand arguing on her fire escape with a crazy kid who has just called her a murderer?

"I don't know what you're talking about," I screamed at him. "I never murdered anybody."

"Oh yes you did," he yelled back, and he opened his

arms, revealing the thing he had cradled against his chest. It was a dying rex begonia.

"But that's just a plant," I told him. "It's just a begonia."

"Just a begonia!" he yelled. "Just a begonia! And you've let it die out here where the temperatures drop into the forties at night. You've starved it and abused it, and the poor thing is dead now, and it's all your fault!"

"Gimme that plant!" I shouted, and pulled it out of his hands. "And get over to your side of the fire escape. If I ever see you over on my side again, I'll . . ."

The boy stopped crying. He looked me straight in the eye, and his voice choked up as he said, "I wouldn't come over to this side of the fire escape for all the money in the world. It's like a morgue here."

Proudly he stood up and walked back to his side of the fire escape and climbed through his window. I put the begonia back with its companions, closed the window, and for the first time in my life, locked it. Then I returned to the kitchen and ate a banana muffin with my father. I knew life would never be the same again for me.

Chapter 4

The next time I saw the boy, I was doing the laundry down in the basement. There are two washing machines and one dryer for the use of all the tenants in our building. Many of them have their own appliances and the others tend to do their laundries over the weekend or in the evenings.

Arthur and I are supposed to share doing the laundry, but for the past year I've taken over the job completely. It's not that Arthur isn't willing—it's just that his talents don't lie in that direction. Maybe it has to do with his sense of democracy—he doesn't like to separate anything, and for a while all of our clothes had the same grayish pink hue and were covered with a fuzzy stubble.

Arthur also used to forget to pull the clothes out of the dryer as soon as they were done, and he never learned how to fold them without including an intricate network of wrinkles that looked like a map of our transit system. When I was younger, I never minded much how my clothes looked, but suddenly, one day shortly after my thirteenth birthday, I caught a glimpse of myself as I was walking along Clement Street with my friends Karen Blue and Jessica Chin. All of us were wearing jeans and tee shirts, but only two of us looked trim and neat. The other one was me.

I spend every Monday afternoon now doing the laundry. Nobody in our building seems to use the washing machines on Monday afternoon, so I've developed a system. Usually there are four loads of laundry, and I am very particular about how they are separated. One is sheets, two is whites, three is coloreds and synthetics and four is towels. If both machines are free I can do two loads at a time. Every so often my mother will run down with a colored turtleneck at the last minute and plead with me to include it. But if the coloreds have been done already, I show no mercy. She can either wait for next week or wash it out by hand. She always waits.

I have also learned how to fold clothes without wrinkling them. I follow Grandmother Cooper's method of dragging clothes out of the dryer as soon as it stops, snapping them vigorously in the air, and laying them out flat on the long drying table in the basement. Then I stand over them like a drill sergeant in an army barracks, and a sense of power rises up inside me. I like the shirts especially. I like to take each one, force its sleeves behind its back, smack down its collar if it has one, and fold it up into a flat, obedient, wrinkle-free square.

My mother feels I take the laundry detail too seriously.

"It doesn't always have to be done on Mondays," she says. "Tuesdays would be just as good."

"No, it wouldn't be," I tell her, "because Mrs. Pincus does her laundry on Tuesdays and Mr. Rogers—he's really flaky. You can never trust him. He's supposed to do his laundry Thursday nights, but sometimes I see him sneaking downstairs on Tuesday afternoons. He just better not try to muscle in on Mondays."

"Really Rebecca," says my mother. "You're taking it all much too seriously. I heard you tell Karen you couldn't go biking because you had to stay home and do the laundry. I don't think it's right for a girl your age to worry about the laundry."

"How come you were listening in to my phone conversation?" I demand.

"I wasn't listening, Rebecca. You know I never actually listen. I was just getting a cup of coffee and I happened to hear you talking."

"Now Mom, I hope you're not going to put all this about my doing the laundry in your book. You promised, Mom, you promised."

"Of course I'm not going to put it in a book. You can't write a book about a girl's first romance and say she spends every Monday afternoon doing the laundry. It sounds weird. My editor would never stand for it."

Laundry #1 and Laundry #2 could be put into the dryer together but Laundry #3 and Laundry #4 had to be separated. On that day Laundry #4 was still in the dryer, and I was inspecting Laundry #3 as it lay spread eagle on the table when I heard footsteps. Now the laundry room in my building is rather dark and dreary, although I had never considered it particularly scary. But when the new boy moved into the room, it suddenly occurred to me that the only way out was through the door he was presently blocking.

When he saw me, his lips actually curled in disgust. He was carrying a blue laundry bag and a box of very cheap detergent. My mother always used to buy that brand until I pointed out to her that only a few cents make the difference between clothes you can be proud of and clothes you wouldn't want your neighbors to think belonged to you.

But my thoughts did not linger on the detergent in his arms. I saw his face turn red, and suddenly he lurched forward. I grabbed a zippered sweat suit jacket for protection and waited for his attack. But no, he had tripped and lay twisting on the floor. Some of his clothes fell out of the duffle bag. I noted with disapproval that they were all mixed up together—towels, jeans and some ladies' nylon underwear. The detergent spilled out on the floor on him, and some of it even ricocheted onto my tennis shoes.

"Yuk!" I yelled.

He didn't say anything. He was crying again, his shoulders heaving up and down, his pale, yellow curls trembling on his head.

"Hey, don't you do anything else besides cry?" I demanded, shaking the cheap detergent off my shoes.

He buried his face in his hands, and you could see the tears forcing their way through his fingers. A lady's slip twisted around a green bathroom mat escaped from the laundry bag.

"You're too old to cry," I said. "You must be at least twelve years old. My brother is only eleven and he hardly ever cries."

That did it. The boy stopped crying and looked at me with hate. "I was fourteen last May," he yelled, "and I don't cry all the time."

"Okay, okay," I told him. "I'm sorry. I didn't really get a good look at you."

He began crying again. "I just hate it here. Everything is going wrong. I wish I were dead." He waved his arm around, indicating the laundry and the spilled detergent. I began feeling sorry for him.

"Here, let me help you," I said. "The washing machines are both free, so we can put in your two loads. You were planning to do two, weren't you?"

"No," he sobbed, "I was going to do only one."

"I mean—the towels and the underwear and the coloreds and the whites? You were going to do them *all* together?"

He stopped crying and looked at me, his mouth open.

"Well, never mind. Here, let's just dump them in together if that's what you want."

I began gathering up the laundry from the floor.

"Just look what I did," the boy said, his voice cracking. "I spilled the whole box of detergent. Oh God, what a mess!"

"Here," I said, "use mine. I know you'll like it. You'll see the difference. It's only a few cents more, but you'll wash those grays away. You won't have to worry what your neighbors think."

"Is this for real?" the boy said.

"What do you mean?"

"I feel like I'm on TV." And suddenly he was grinning at me.

"I don't know what you're talking about," I said coldly.

"I mean, the way you were just talking about your detergent. It sounded like a TV commercial." He began laughing. "You're really very good."

"But it's true," I told him. "This is the best laundry detergent on the market." I held up a grimy kitchen towel from his pile on the floor. "No other detergent can get the grime out the way this one can. Just wait and see."

"Stop it! Stop it!" the boy yelled and doubled over with laughter.

"Stop what?" I shouted.

"Oh God!" he said. "You're a natural. I never heard anything so funny in my whole life."

I waited for him to stop laughing. I was going to tell him in my icy voice exactly what he could do with his laundry when suddenly he raised his head, stopped laughing and said in a high voice, "I'm sorry."

"You should be," I told him.

"I don't mean because I spilled the detergent on you. I mean because of the way I acted the other day."

"Oh that!" I said.

"I guess you really didn't mean to kill that rex begonia. I guess you just didn't understand how to take care of it. I'm sorry I carried on like that, but it was just the final straw. Everything in my life is upside down and when I saw that plant . . ."

I didn't tell him then how many plants of ours had expired out on the fire escape. I didn't say anything about plants at all as we finished gathering up the laundry from the floor and putting it into the machine. When he stood up I saw that he was very slim and rather short, at least half a head shorter than I. He had far too much laundry in one machine, and I shuddered as I watched him add an Indian madras apron (not colorfast of course) to a bunch of whitish pillowcases. But I didn't want to say anything further on the subject of laundry. The boy used some of my detergent, and then I helped him sweep up his mess on the floor.

"Thanks," he said when we finished. "Uh . . ."

"Well . . ." I said. Both of us suddenly turned embarrassed and uncomfortable with each other. I didn't know what to say next, and I guess he didn't either. Laundry #3 still lay stretched out on the table, and I began moving towards it.

"Um . . . I . . . um . . . I'm chasingfirst," he said finally.

"What?"

"I said my name is Jason Furst," he repeated.

"Oh, well, I'm Rebecca Cooper." I picked up a lavender turtleneck shirt of my mother's and gave it a hard snap in the air.

"Let me help you," Jason offered. He grabbed one of my father's shirts and began folding it with its collar crumpled and its sleeves twisted up sideways. I had to stop him. Desperately, I began talking.

"I'm the one who does the laundry in my family. How about you? Do you do the laundry in yours?"

His face began quivering again.

"Never mind," I said quickly. "Here, don't bother with that. Why don't we just sit down and talk for a while?" I took a pair of my jeans away from him which he had been misfolding knees up.

"I hate doing the laundry," he said. "I never had to do it in Santa Monica."

"Oh, is that where you're from?" I led him away from my laundry to the bench across from the dryer.

"It's like a bad dream," he said, his eyes wild. "I keep thinking I'm going to wake up and I'll be back home."

"What do you mean?"

His face began twisting up again.

"Don't cry," I said. "Why don't we talk about something else?"

"No, no," he insisted, gulping, "I want to talk about it. I have to talk about it. She won't tell me the truth. She's lying. I know she's lying."

"You mean your mother?"

"She doesn't want me to talk to anybody else either. I keep telling her I know she's not telling me the truth, but she gets angry. She doesn't want me to talk about it. She's a different person. She never used to be like this."

There was the sound of the elevator door banging and quick footsteps hurrying towards the laundry room.

"My mother!" the boy whispered nervously. "She said I shouldn't talk to anybody in your family. She thinks you're all snoopy."

"But . . . but . . . why?" I stammered.

"Look in the begonia," he said quickly as his mother came running into the room.

Her face reddened when she saw me and she snapped at her son, "What took you so long?"

"I . . . I . . . fell," he said. "I . . . she . . . helped me pick the laundry up."

"Well, why are you sitting here now? I told you to come right up again. I told you!"

The boy rose. His head drooped, and he moved slowly towards the door. The woman looked at me, eyes narrowed and lips tightly pressed against her teeth. When he reached her, she put a thin hand with long, dark fingernails on his shoulder and pulled him out of the room.

Chapter 5

My mother was having trouble with *First Love.*

"It's just that I'm not sure how a boy nowadays goes about asking for a date."

"The ones I know don't," I told her.

"Well, see, that's what I mean. When I was a girl, a boy would call you up and ask you to go out with him. Maybe you'd go bowling or to a movie, and after, you might go for an ice-cream soda. If he couldn't afford it . . ."

"What do you mean if he couldn't afford it? Nowadays, each one pays his or her own way. I mean, I would if anybody asked me."

"I know that," said my mother, "but I really need to know how boys and girls communicate with each other. I never *hear* boys and girls talking to each other, especially over the phone." She looked at me mournfully.

"Well I'm sorry, but there's nothing I can do about that."

"Maybe you can ask some of your friends."

"Like who?"

"Karen."

"She likes boys, but things aren't any better with

her than with me. Once she found a boy's wallet in the hall. His name was Jeffrey Morgan and she called him up. He told her to leave it in the Lost and Found, so she never even got to meet him."

"Mmm," said my mother. "That would make a good story. A girl finds a boy's wallet, and they talk over the phone back and forth and finally they meet and . . ."

"And what?"

"Well, I don't know yet, but meanwhile I need to get the feel of teenage conversations. Don't you know anybody who goes out with boys?"

"Jessica went out once with a boy named Rodney Lucas. But then he moved away and he sent her a Christmas card. There is a girl in my class, Rosemary Jenkins. Everybody says she sleeps around, but I guess I could ask her."

"No, no, I want a girl who's a virgin. She has to be a virgin. That's the new look in teenage books. It's only the old-fashioned ones where the kids are sleeping together. But I just wish I could listen in to a boy and a girl talking on the phone together. I wish I could even listen to a teenage girl talking on the phone."

She meant me because I never say anything important over the phone. I know she's likely to be patrolling and I want to keep my private affairs out of her books.

I had the fire escape all to myself again. Jason Furst had vanished. So had his mother. Right after our meeting in the laundry room, he simply disappeared. I sat out on my fire escape and wondered what had happened to him. It was wonderful having the fire escape all to myself again and I tried not to worry. But after what I had seen down in the laundry room, I couldn't help feeling there was something very strange going on and that Jason's mother was up to no good.

On the day following our meeting, I checked the dying begonia plant, but there was no message. I sat out on the fire escape, studying and enjoying my solitude. I didn't want to have to worry about Jason. In a way it would be the best thing if he and his mother simply disappeared—for good. But I worried. Carefully, I inched myself over to Jason's window and peeked inside. There were no shades or drapes up and I could see everything. There were no people in the room, but there were plants—many, many plants—big ones, little ones, flowering ones—all lush and green and healthy. There was nothing else in the room—only plants.

I moved back to my side of the fire escape and considered. Should I call the police? Should I tell them I suspected foul play—that Jason Furst and his mother, or the woman he said was his mother, had disappeared? I remembered her clawlike hands with their long, blood red fingernails gripping his shoulder. I remembered his fear when he heard her footsteps down in the basement.

The weather was so beautiful, I decided to wait another day.

It was beautiful on the next day too, so I decided to wait one more. The weather was supposed to turn foggy and cold, anyway.

Thursday afternoon, I hurried home from school, threw open the window and eased myself down to Jason's window. It was a particularly blowy day, and I shivered in the cold wind. I looked through Jason's window. A face looked back at me. It was Jason's mother's face. She opened the window and snapped, "What are you doing?"

"Oh," I said, "I always sit out on the fire escape. I was just . . . uh . . . doing my homework."

"You were looking in my window," she snarled.

"Well, I guess I just made a mistake. I guess I . . ."

"I guess you just better mind your own business," she said, and slammed the window shut.

I retreated to my side of the fire escape. If Jason's mother had returned, where was Jason? I started nibbling on the nail of my right pinky. I always chew on that pinky when I'm nervous. All my other nails are full grown but not the one on my right pinky. Every so often when there's nothing left to chew on that nail, I try the one on my left pinky, but that's only in an emergency. It doesn't really taste as good. Usually I try to leave a little leftover scrap of nail or cuticle for another day. But on that Thursday, I was devouring every chewable speck as I deliberated on what my next move should be.

Of course! The telephone! Wasn't that the way teenagers of my generation communicated? The trouble was my mother might be lurking somewhere in the vicinity waiting to hear my conversation. But I couldn't help it this time. I would call his number and ask for him. If he was there, his mother would have to let me talk to him. Or would she? What would I do if she refused to let me speak to him?

I chewed off a last comforting nail fragment from my pinky, pulled my finger out of my mouth and began climbing back through my window. That's when I saw it, sticking up in the flowerpot, right to one side of the brown, withered rex begonia. It was a tightly rolled scrap of paper.

I opened it and read:

Can you meet me in front of
the conservatory of flowers
in Golden Gate Park at 4 on Friday?
J.

I turned the paper over and wrote:

Yes.
R.

Then I folded the note and stuck it back into the flowerpot. Although I sat out on my side of the fire escape the rest of that cold, foggy afternoon, I did not see Jason.

But the next morning, when I pulled up the shade, the note was gone.

Usually on Friday afternoons, Karen Blue comes over to my house and spends the night or I go over to Karen's house. She wasn't in school on Friday, but when I got home my mother told me she had called and wanted me to call back. The clock said three fifteen, so I didn't have a whole lot of time. I quickly dialed her number.

"Hello," I said. "Karen?"

"Yes. Rebecca?"

"Uh huh. What happened to you today?"

"Oh, I have an infected toe and it hurts when I walk on it. You better come over to my house today."

"Okay, but I'll have to come later."

"Why?"

"I'll tell you when I see you. I gotta run now. Good-bye."

"Good-bye."

As soon as I hung up, the phone rang again. It was Karen.

"You didn't say what time you were coming," she said.

"Oh well, maybe about six—I'm not sure."

"My mother's making a soufflé. She needs to know exactly."

"Better make it seven just to be on the safe side."

"Okay, but where are you going?"

"I really don't want to say. Not now! Later, I'll tell you."

"What's the big mystery? You've been acting kind of funny lately. Does it have anything to do with that crazy family next door?"

"I don't want to say."

"I tell you everything, Rebecca, and you never tell me anything."

"I do so tell you everything, but I can't tell you *now* over the phone. You know why."

"You mean because your mother's listening?"

"Uh huh."

"Okay, but promise you'll tell me later."

"I promise."

"How about giving me a hint?"

"I can't, and besides, I'm late. I've got to go. Will you please stop talking to me?"

"You stink, Rebecca."

"So do you. Good-bye."

My mother was drinking one of her innumerable cups of coffee, and she followed me into my room and sat on my bed as I threw a few things into my back-pack.

"Going over to Karen's house today?"

"Yes, Mom. I'll bike over, and I guess I'll spend the night."

"How is Karen?"

"She's got an infected toe, but otherwise she's fine."

"Anything new with Karen?"

"No, I don't think so, Mom."

"And you, Rebecca? Anything new with you?"

"Nothing special, Mom." My mother looked sadly into her cup of coffee and I said quickly, "Uh . . . how's the book, Mom?"

My mother shook her head. "A few problems I'd like to talk over with you."

It was three thirty-five and I had to meet Jason over at the conservatory by four.

"Maybe we can talk about it tomorrow when I get back," I told her. "I've got to go now, Mom."

My mother looked disappointed, but she didn't try to stop me as I hurried out of the room.

Jason was already there when I arrived. He was sitting on the steps leading up to the conservatory. This was the third time that I had seen him, but only the first time that he wasn't crying. He smiled when he saw me as I carried my bike up the stairs towards him.

"Where have you been for the past few days?" I demanded.

"Over at Alice's—my mother's friend. My mother had to go away for a few days."

"Well, I was worried about you. I was afraid something had happened to you."

"What?"

He opened his eyes wide. They were startling

eyes—almost black in his pale face under all that pale hair.

"I don't know what," I said crankily, "but I was nervous because of the way your mother yanked you out of the laundry room. And then you were gone all those days."

"Only three," he said.

"Well, I wasn't sure what to do. If you had been gone another day, I was thinking of calling the police."

"We couldn't have been gone another day," he said, "because the plants needed to be watered."

"Well, I didn't know that, and then your mother . . . Look, Jason, can I ask you a question?"

"Sure."

"Is she really your mother?"

Jason shook his head and shuddered. As if he were trying to shake off some chilling, icy water at the back of his neck. "My mother?" he said. His eyes moved away from me, down the stairs to the lively, formal beds of bright autumn flowers that stretched out on the field below the conservatory. Suddenly, he stretched out a finger and pointed. I followed it and saw a plump, white bunny moving through the flowers. It was like out of a painting—the soft, beautiful white rabbit, surrounded by bright clumps of gold and orange and winey red. In the midst of all our problems and fears, I reflected, how beautiful the creatures of the world were and how good it was to be alive.

Jason leaped to his feet, and before I could murmur my admiration of the scene below us, he dashed down the stairs, flew at the bunny and aimed a kick at its fluffy cottontail. The rabbit went bounding off through the flower beds, across the lawn and disappeared finally into the bushes. Jason returned, his face red with outrage.

"Did you see that?" he shouted.

"I certainly did, and I thought it was disgraceful."

"It certainly is disgraceful," Jason said. "Those lamebrained people who turn their rabbits loose in the park because they don't want to take care of them any-more . . . disgusting . . . filthy slobs!"

"You mean the people who turn them loose?"

"No, no, the rabbits. They're disgusting. They eat any plant in sight. They destroy everything they wrap their teeth around. Did you see that one chewing on the dahlias? I got him just in time. He would have eaten every marigold in sight if I hadn't chased him away. But he'll be back. You can be sure of that."

"You tried to kick him."

"I'd like to kill him," Jason said. "And I'd like to kill the person who turned him loose too. When I think of all the rare plants he's probably going to destroy . . ."

"But a rabbit has as much right to live as a plant," I said.

Jason looked at me as if I were crazy.

"I mean who are you to decide that a dahlia is more important than a rabbit? As far as I'm concerned, I *like* rabbits better than dahlias."

"I like rabbits too," Jason said, "especially in a mus-tard sauce."

"You *eat* rabbits?" I said.

"Sure I eat rabbits," said Jason. "That's the only way I like them. The best kind of rabbit is a dead rab-bit."

"But that's disgusting," I insisted.

"Rabbits are disgusting," said Jason. "But they get

a good press. All this business about the Easter Bunny and Peter Rabbit and Flopsy, Mopsy and Cotton-tail. That's the trouble. They don't tell you how rabbits will eat anything—anything. You can spend years developing a beautiful, rare plant, and in a matter of a few minutes, a rabbit can destroy a whole life's work. Anybody who loves plants hates rabbits."

"Well," said I, "then I'm glad I don't love plants."

"Where's the gardener?" Jason yelled, looking around. "Come on, let's go find the gardener."

I followed along after him, dragging my bike with me up the stairs. But I kept right on talking. I wasn't finished telling him what I thought of him. What I thought of anyone who would kill a cute, little, helpless bunny.

He wasn't listening, I knew that. He was looking for the gardener and he hurried through the entrance to the conservatory of flowers with me right behind him, giving him a good piece of my mind.

The conservatory smelled heavy with the fragrance of flowers and green things. My family and I had trooped through a number of times in the past whenever there didn't seem anything better to do. Jason headed around the inner court, past the large banana tree when suddenly—

"Jason," I whispered. "Listen, Jason!"

He stopped and so did I as the sound of a woman's heels came clicking around the path behind us. I tried to push him behind me, to shield him from her. I put my bike up against my chest to barricade the two of us as the sound of his mother's footsteps came closer and closer.

Chapter 6

"Stop!" she yelled, even before she moved into sight. "Stop!"

"Don't worry," I said to Jason. "I won't let her hurt you this time."

The woman came bounding around the path, and the leaves of the banana plant swayed.

"Just stop!"

It was not Jason's mother. It was a woman gardener, a large, round one, and she was pointing a finger at me. "You . . . you . . . get that bike out of here this minute," she said. "Didn't you see the sign up outside? No bikes in the conservatory!"

"It's my fault," said Jason, emerging from behind me. "I wasn't thinking, ma'am, but do you work here?"

"Yes."

"Well, I didn't notice the sign because I was too upset. Somebody has turned a pet rabbit loose and I saw him down in the dahlias. He was eating a Victoria Hodgkiss dahlia."

"A Victoria Hodgkiss dahlia!" said the woman, her voice trembling.

"I'm afraid so," Jason said grimly. "I chased it away but I'm sure it will return."

The woman's eyes narrowed. "We'll get it," she said. "Don't worry—we'll get it if I have to use everyone on my staff. This will be the thirteenth rabbit that's been turned loose since Easter, and I only wish we could catch the owners."

Jason made sympathetic clucking noises. Then he said, "I used to live in Santa Monica, and you should see what one of them did to my collection of tuberous begonias. Are you familiar with tuberous begonias?"

"Am I familiar with tuberous begonias?" said the gardener. "Did you see the display we have in the west wing? It's nearly ready to come down, but I set it up."

"Is that so?"

"Yes, and I've done a book and several pamphlets on begonias."

"What's your name?" cried Jason.

"Irene Cummings."

"Not *the* Irene Cummings! Not the Irene Cummings who developed the Smoky Flamingo variety of tuberous begonia!"

The woman's chubby face grew pink. "Well," she said, "I did work on that one with my late husband, may he rest in peace."

Jason said in a hushed voice, "I've wanted to meet you for years. I've just moved up here from Santa Monica. I belonged to the Begonia Society down there and your last pamphlet was an absolute bible to us—I want you to know—an absolute bible."

"That's very kind of you to say," said Irene Cummings, giggling modestly, "and it certainly is a pleasure meeting you—uh . . ."

"Jason Furst."

"Jason Furst."

They stood there, smiling into each other's eyes.

"I'd love to see that display of begonias," Jason said softly, and the two of them turned and walked off together into the interior of the hothouse.

About half an hour later he returned. Irene Cummings accompanied him to the entrance, where the two of them shook hands. Jason looked as if he had just come out of the promised land.

"She invited me to join the Begonia Society up here. She also said she would take me on a personal tour of the hothouses in back and is going to write out a formula for—"

"Do you know I've been sitting out here waiting for you for over half an hour?" I said.

"Oh God!" Jason said, his face collapsing. "I'm sorry. I forgot all about you."

"Thanks a lot," I told him. "It's been quite a day for me. I came here to help somebody out who I think is in trouble. I see him kick a rabbit and make friends with a lady who knows everything there is to know about tumorous begonias. . . ."

"Tuberous," Jason corrected. "And she doesn't know everything. She didn't know that a little horse manure mixed with a fish emulsion—"

"I don't want to hear any of this," I said, pulling up my bike. "I've been sitting here waiting for you, and I'm cold and disgusted, and it doesn't seem to me that you need any help at all. If anybody needs help, it's that poor rabbit."

"No," said Jason, his eyes filling with tears. "I do need help."

We sat on the steps leading to the conservatory and Jason told me his story. The white rabbit did not appear again so we were not interrupted.

"Up until two months ago," Jason said, "my life was

perfect. My mother was everything a mother could be, and my father . . . my father . . ." His voice trembled.

"If you start crying again," I said, "I'm just going to get up and walk away."

"I'm not crying," Jason said, straightening up and fastening his eyes on my face. Incredible eyes they were, very dark with the saddest look I had ever seen, sadder even than the look in my father's eyes on weekends.

"My father and I were more than just father and son," Jason continued. "I was his only child, and we've been close ever since I can remember."

"Does he like begonias too?" I asked.

"Does he like begonias!" said Jason. "He was the one who got me interested. My father could have been a great botanist. You should have seen our garden in Santa Monica. There was nothing he couldn't grow, no plant that did not blossom under his care. We had our own little hothouse in the back, and every weekend my father and I worked together on many different kinds of plants, but most often the tuberous begonia."

"And your mother?" I asked carefully. "What about your mother?"

"My mother's interests lie more in African violets, which you may have noticed that day she caught you looking in the window."

"I was looking for *you*," I told him severely. "I didn't notice what kind of plants there were."

"Well, my mother was always more interested in indoor plants, unlike my father and me." His voice faltered again.

"Jason!" I warned.

He sighed and continued. "My father always hoped that I would grow up to become a botanist. It had been the disappointment of his life that he had never been able to become a botanist himself. He was a poor boy, and he had to leave college and go to work. My father always did very well. He started his own business, manufacturing dental supplies. We had plenty of money, a big house and enough means to afford vacations to many of the famous gardens of the world."

"Sounds like a lot of fun," I said, "but let's get back to your mother."

"My mother!" Jason said, looking off into space. "Suddenly she changed."

"Ah!" said I. "How?"

"My mother was always the perfect mother. Our house shone, our meals were delicious and she encouraged my father and me in all our botanical pursuits."

"But what did she do? I mean, did she work?"

"No, of course not. She didn't have to. She stayed home and took care of the house and her family."

"You sound like a sexist, Jason Furst," I told him.

"Do I?" he said, surprised. "That's interesting."

"I don't think it's very interesting," I said, "but go on, go on."

"My mother was also always overweight. She made wonderful meals and gained weight more easily than the two of us."

"Your mother overweight? That skinny lady?"

"Yes—it all happened suddenly. In a couple of months, my mother lost thirty or forty pounds and our whole world collapsed around our ears."

"Well, so tell me—what happened?"

"I don't know what happened," said Jason Furst, "but suddenly one day, my father kissed me and told me to take care of my mother. He never told me to take care of my mother before. Sometimes, he told me to spray some of the fruit trees in our garden, or repot some seedlings, but never, never did he tell me to take care of my mother."

"You became suspicious?"

"No, not then. I asked him where he was going. He hesitated and then said he needed to go abroad. His face clouded when he said it. It would be a business trip, he said, an extended one, and he might need to be away for some time. I didn't worry then. My father had made trips abroad before. He had business with firms in Austria, France, and Switzerland. Sometimes he had been gone for a month or two, and each time he had returned with interesting seeds gathered on his travels."

"What did your mother say?"

"My mother didn't say anything. But she began crying. Right after he left, she began crying, and for another week, all she did was cry. I was confused and disturbed. I showed her all the buds developing on our tuberous begonias, but it only made her cry all the more. But I still didn't worry until she began neglecting her African violets. Then I knew something was seriously wrong."

"What happened next?"

"We got a card from my father in Paris."

"What did it say?"

"It said, *Very disappointing flower beds in the Jardin des Tuileries. Miss you both very much. Love, Dad.*"

"And then what happened?"

"My mother went wild. Especially after Mrs. Ferguson, our next door neighbor, asked me to come into her garden and look at her compost pile. She stopped crying and she began packing. She said we had to move. She said she was going to sell the house and that we'd never come back again. I kept asking her why. But she wouldn't tell me. I could see that she was frightened even though she said she wasn't. I asked her what about Dad, and she said he would join us in San Francisco. She said we had to go to San Francisco. I told her that most of our plants would never survive the climate change, and she said . . . she said . . ."

"Steady now, Jason, steady!"

"She said we could only take the ones that would."

I sat thinking about what Jason had said. There had to be a clue lost somewhere in the midst of all those flowering plants.

"Tell me again what your father's card said," I asked him.

"It said, *Very disappointing flower beds in the Jardin des Tuileries. Miss you very much. Love, Dad.*"

"Hmm," I said. "It must be something that he said in that card."

"But what?" cried Jason.

"So anyway, go on."

"Well, we came up here about a month ago and stayed with an old friend of my mother's. My mother kept disappearing for a couple of days every week while I stayed with Alice. Then, last week, she decided we needed our own place and here we are."

"But this week, she also disappeared for a few days, didn't she?"

"That's right. She won't tell me where she's going. She keeps saying it has something to do with Dad's business."

"Where is your father's business?"

Jason hesitated. "It was in Los Angeles. Before the

fire, I mean. The whole building burned down. My father will have to find a new place when he gets back."

"Well, I guess that's where she goes—to Los Angeles. She must have a lot of business details to work out."

"I figured that out too, but why won't she take me with her?"

"That's right. You'd like to see your friends."

"What friends? I never had any friends except for the people in the Begonia Society. There is a dentist I wouldn't mind getting in touch with. He's developing a black tuberous begonia, but . . ."

"You mean you don't have any friends your own age?"

"No," said Jason, "I don't. My mother used to say it was because I was so much smarter than most kids my age."

"Mothers always think you're smarter," I said.

"Does your mother think you're smarter?" asked Jason.

"She knows I'm smarter," I told him. "She doesn't like it, but there's nothing either one of us can do about it. I guess I've never had lots of friends, but I always have some. How come you've never had any?"

"I just haven't," said Jason. "But as long as I had my father, it didn't seem to matter."

"Well, I think you could use some friends your own age too," I told him.

He was looking at me now, questioningly.

"I don't know, Jason," I told him. "I don't know if we're types. I felt very sorry for you down in the basement the other day, and now that I've heard your story, I still feel sorry for you and I'd like to help you, but . . ."

"I'd like to be your friend," he said in a pathetic voice. "I don't even mind if you kill begonias."

"Well, and I guess I can put up with you kicking rabbits, if you don't do it when I'm around."

Jason nodded. "I don't know what to do next," he said. "What do you think I should do next?"

"Well, I think we have to figure out what really happened to your father. You don't really think he's on a business trip to Europe, do you?"

Jason shook his head. "Not anymore, I don't."

"Okay, let's consider the possibilities. Number one, Jason, did you ever consider that your father might work for the CIA?"

"My father? Are you crazy?"

"No, no, listen to me. You said yourself that he's always made a number of trips to Europe, right? It seems very likely to me that he's always worked for the CIA, but obviously he couldn't let you know."

"And my mother?"

"Your mother, of course, knew it and she also understood something in that card he sent you from Paris. Something in code that made her frightened."

"But what?"

"I don't know what, but suddenly you say she changed. Suddenly you had to move away, sell your house, leave the old neighborhood."

"But why would we have to do that?"

"Don't you see—because he tipped her off to something. Something dangerous. Maybe he's on a secret mission and he doesn't want anybody to know where the two of you are."

Jason scratched his head. "No," he said, "you don't know my father. He doesn't look like a CIA agent. All he knows about is plants and dental supplies."

"But that's just it," I said. "He'd be perfect for the CIA if he didn't look like a regular CIA agent. You're not supposed to look like a CIA agent. Don't you ever watch TV?"

"Very seldom," Jason said. "My father never approved of TV unless it was a program on plants or maybe whales. He also didn't mind programs on art."

"There!" I said triumphantly. "That's it. He didn't want you to know what was going on. He wanted to keep you ignorant, just fiddling around with plants. Don't you see, Jason, what's been happening while you've been potting your seedlings?"

"I didn't have a chance to," he said sadly. "My mother yanked me away from Santa Monica so fast I didn't even have a chance to give my plants away. It was a terrible tragedy. Hundreds of rare plants . . ."

"Jason, will you please concentrate on what I'm saying to you?"

Jason shook his head and began shivering. He was dressed in a light jacket, not at all appropriate for a late San Francisco afternoon with the fog rolling in.

"You're going to have to get some warmer clothes for San Francisco," I told him. "It gets cold up here, especially in the late afternoon."

Jason looked at his watch and jumped up. "I've got to get home. She thinks I'm at the library. I'm not supposed to be here with you. She said I shouldn't talk to anybody in your family. I've got to get home."

"Well, okay, Jason. It's just as well. I want to think all this over, and maybe something else will occur to me."

"I've got to go," Jason said. "I was supposed to be home by five and it's nearly six."

"Well, okay," I said, standing up and straightening my bike.

Jason was digging frantically through his pockets.

"What's the matter?"

"I don't have any money to get home."

"How come you didn't take your bike?"

"I never learned how to ride one. Have you got any money?"

"About forty cents."

"Well, you better give it to me. I need bus fare, and maybe I'll pick up a candy bar. I'm getting hungry."

"You have to pay it back though."

"Sure I'll pay it back," he said. "I'll put it in the begonia plant next time I leave you a note. Maybe tomorrow. Look there tomorrow."

Chapter 7 ❦

Karen Blue's mother did not make a soufflé for dinner. She was too busy fighting with Karen Blue's father. Unlike my parents, who fight all over the house, Karen's parents usually go into their bedroom, lock the door and go at each other there.

"Ma!" Karen yelled, knocking at the door, "I'm starving, Ma. When are we going to eat?"

"In a few minutes, dear," Karen's mother called back.

"Rebecca's here and she's starving too."

"That's all right, Mrs. Blue," I called out. "I can wait."

Karen's mother opened the bedroom door. She was breathing hard and her face was sort of a deep purple. So was Mr. Blue's face. He was standing over a broken ashtray, and there was a white smack mark on one of his purple cheeks.

"How are you, Rebecca?" said Mrs. Blue.

"Just fine, Mrs. Blue. And you?"

"Just fine."

"How are you, Mr. Blue?" I called.

"Couldn't be better." Mr. Blue smiled and waved a hand at me. "How are your parents, Rebecca?"

"Just fine, Mr. Blue. My father cut his finger last night while he was slicing carrots, and my mother thinks he should have gone to the hospital for a few stitches, but he says it will heal by itself."

"Well," said Mr. Blue gravely, "most things heal by themselves. Not everything though."

"That's right," said Mrs. Blue. "Not everything."

Mr. Blue stirred the broken pieces of ashtray with his foot and nodded solemnly.

"I'm starving, Ma," Karen said. "When are we eating?"

"Where's Lisa?" asked Mrs. Blue.

"She and Heidi are over at Aunt Bev's. Don't you remember, Mom? She's taking them for haircuts at that haircutting school where they only charge five dollars. Then they're going to eat dinner at that chef's college where you can eat as much as you like for three dollars and seventy-five cents."

"Why don't you start making a salad and I'll be out in a few minutes." Mrs. Blue began to close the door again.

"Ma!" Karen yelled. "I've got an infected toe, Ma. I shouldn't even be standing. Stop fighting with Daddy for a while. Just until after dinner."

Mrs. Blue opened the door halfway. "Daddy and I aren't fighting, dear," she said. "Just because we aren't agreeing doesn't mean we're fighting."

"I can make dinner, Mrs. Blue," I offered. "My father made a delicious meal on Thursday, after he cut his finger, with carrots, yogurt, tuna fish and raisins. It sounds weird but it really tastes great. Especially with sweet potatoes. Do you have any sweet potatoes, Mrs. Blue?"

"I'm afraid not," she said, opening the door all the way. "It's really too bad because I'm sure we'd all love your father's recipe. Harry!" Mrs. Blue turned her head slightly and addressed her left shoulder. "We'll have to finish our discussion later."

Mr. and Mrs. Blue returned to the bedroom after dinner, and I stacked the dishes in the dishwasher. Karen said she had to stay off her infected toe. She sat in the kitchen with one foot up on a chair.

"Well," she said, "where were you?"

"In the park."

"Who with?"

"Jason Furst."

"That's the boy next door?"

"Uh huh."

"The little shrimpy kid who cries all the time?"

"Uh huh."

"I want to hear all about it," Karen said in a bored voice, and began peeling the bandages off her infected toe.

"What are you doing that for?" I asked her.

"Don't you want to see what it looks like?"

"Not particularly."

"Well, I do. The doctor had to drain all the pus off, and I'm supposed to soak it anyway. If you don't mind, Rebecca, put some water up to boil and bring me that white basin under the sink."

"I thought you wanted to hear about Jason Furst."

"I do, I do." Karen said, inspecting her toe. "Just look at it, Rebecca. It's still all red and inflamed. I wonder if I'll be able to stay out of school on Monday."

"I doubt it," I told her. "It will probably feel much better by tomorrow."

"Why do you say that?" Karen said. "Timmy Kronberg had an infected toe that got worse. They even considered amputating it."

"Timmy who?"

"Kronberg. He's in my Spanish class. His toe turned blue, and he said the pus was kind of green." Karen bent all the way over so she could really see her toe. "I don't think mine is green though."

"Listen, Karen, getting back to Jason Furst . . ."

"Mine is more yellow. But Timmy Kronberg said his started out yellow. That was before his toe turned blue."

"Something very mysterious is happening to Jason's father and . . ."

Karen left off examining her toe and looked up at me. "Aren't you interested in how I know so much about Timmy Kronberg's toe? I thought you'd want to know."

"Well, yes, but I thought you . . ."

Karen began giggling. "It really is odd how both of us had infected toes. I mean I always felt we had a lot in common. I called him this afternoon, after I spoke to you, and we talked for two hours, and he said . . ."

It's a funny thing about Karen. She always asks me lots of questions, but she usually isn't interested in hearing the answers. Like this afternoon, on the phone. She really seemed very interested in where I was going and what I was doing. I couldn't tell her anything because my mother was patrolling, and maybe it's those times when I can't answer questions that Karen is most interested in asking them.

Karen told me everything she and Timmy discussed during their phone conversation and admitted that she had a crush on him.

"I thought you liked Doug McIntyre."

"Well, I used to but not anymore. Anyway, Timmy said he's going to call me tomorrow, and maybe I'll ask him to drop over. He's real tall—just a freshman like us, but he's on the football team already and he has curly, dark hair just like the boy in *New Boy in Town*."

"I didn't read that one yet."

"Oh, you'll love it. I'll lend it to you. If you like, you can read it tonight. I'm reading *A Boyfriend for Linda*. It's by the same author, but it's not as good. The boy has blond hair and I don't like boys with blond hair. That boy who lives next door to you has blond hair, doesn't he?"

"Very pale blond hair, almost white."

"Yuk! I don't know how you can like somebody like that."

"I don't like him. I mean, he's just a friend. I mean—cut it out, Karen, he's not my boyfriend. He's just a kid who needs a friend."

"Well," said Karen, "he doesn't sound like my type at all."

I finally managed to tell Karen about Jason and his father, but she didn't seem very interested. Then we both read our books, and later Karen put polish on her nine good toenails and talked some more about Timmy Kronberg.

My mother was waiting for me when I arrived home from Karen's the next morning.

"I'm taking you out to lunch," she said.

"How come?" I asked suspiciously.

"Oh, it's such a beautiful day," she said. "Arthur is off playing ball with his friends. Dad is working, poor thing, and it's been ages since the two of us had lunch together."

"It's the book," I said. "You're having trouble with the book."

"Well," she admitted, "I wouldn't mind just checking out a few things with you. But where would you like to go?"

"How about Zacks?" I said. "We haven't been there in a long time."

"Dad has the car," said my mother, "but we could bike over if you like. I could use a little exercise."

Zacks is in Sausalito, across the Golden Gate Bridge. There was a strong wind blowing and my mother kept falling behind. I'd stop and wait for her and she'd come pedaling up, huffing and puffing. "I'm just out of shape," she said breathlessly, "or maybe I'm just too old."

"Forty's not really old," I said kindly. My mother's cheeks were very pink and her blue eyes full of shiny lights. We look a lot alike, even down to the freckles all over our faces and our blonde hair. Hers is beginning to turn gray, but if you don't get too close to her and squint a little, she looks much younger.

"Do you think you can make it, Mom? Maybe we should turn back."

"No, no, but let's just stop for a minute and admire the view."

It was worth admiring. Down in the bay, all the little white sailboats skimmed over the bright blue waters. The city gleamed sharp and clear in the sunshine. My mother put an arm around my shoulder, and I leaned my head against hers. How lucky I was to live in this beautiful place and have such a marvelous mother!

But an hour later, sitting in Zacks and eating our hamburgers out on the deck over the bay as the sea gulls whirled around us, I was shouting at her.

"You've done it again," I cried. "You just won't stop."

"Just because Melanie likes to do her homework out on the fire escape—lots of people—"

"No, they don't—and I want that girl off my fire escape."

"Okay, Rebecca, okay. Calm down. It's not your fire escape, but okay, we'll leave out all of the fire escape parts."

"I want her to do her homework inside. Do you hear, Mom? Inside, on an oak or teak desk with a picture of some punk rocker hanging on her wall."

"Of course, darling," said my mother meekly, "of course. Now can we go on?"

I took another bite of my hamburger and glared at her.

"It's the boy I'm really having trouble with."

Some ketchup dribbled out of my hamburger and onto my shirt. As I rubbed at it, my mother continued.

"He's a little wooden, I think, and I don't know what to do with him."

"What's his name?"

"Jason."

"What?" I yelled. "Why is his name Jason?"

My mother's blue eyes opened very wide. "What's the matter with Jason?"

"You know very well what's the matter. It's the name of the kid next door."

My mother scrunched up her face.

"You're doing it again. You know I don't like you to use my friends' names in your books."

"But I didn't know he was your friend," my mother said reproachfully. "I didn't even know his name was Jason. You never told me you knew him."

I began rubbing at the spot on my shirt again.

"You never tell me anything," said my mother.

"Well, I'm telling you now, Mom. Please don't use his name."

My mother sighed. "All right, Rebecca, what should I call him?"

"I don't care— Henry—why don't you call him Henry?"

"Nobody calls anybody Henry anymore. I can't call him Henry."

"How about David? That's a good name for a boy."

"Hmmm— David," my mother said. "David . . . Dave . . . Davey."

"Not Davey," I said. "David or Dave."

"Really, Rebecca, he's my character. I'll call him anything I like. As long as it isn't a name of somebody you like."

"I didn't say I liked Jason. I just don't want the boy called Jason."

"I'm not calling him David," said my mother. "I don't like David. I'm in the mood for a name with *J*. Maybe Jim. You don't like any Jims do you?"

"No, I don't and I don't like the name either."

"That's fine," said my mother. "His name is Jim then. But that's not really what I want to talk about. His name isn't really important. It's him, Jim. Something's wrong with him."

"What is it?" I fed some pieces of my hamburger bun to a couple of friendly sea gulls and wondered what Jason thought of sea gulls.

"That's just it. There's nothing wrong with him. He's a nice boy, good-looking too."

"What does he look like?"

"Well, he's about six feet, dark hair and dark eyes

with a nice kind of crooked smile and good teeth."

"He sounds like a horse," I said, hooking a piece of onion with a french fry.

"He's a manly boy and he loves animals. As a matter of fact, I think he'll be planning to be a vet when he grows up." My mother brightened. "Maybe I could have Melanie plan to be a vet too. The two of them could have their love of animals in common."

"Why do the boys always have to be tall and good-looking in books?" I asked my mother.

"I suppose," said my mother, "because girls like to read about good-looking boys."

"That's not the way it is in life," I said. "There aren't very many tall, handsome, manly boys. There was one in my history class last year, but he lisped when he talked, and then there was Alex Ritter, but he was always combing his hair."

"Would you read a book about a boy who wasn't good-looking?" my mother asked, smiling at a bold sea gull that had perched at the edge of our table.

"I don't know," I told her. "I do like them good-looking in books. I just wish there were more of them in real life."

My mother and I talked for a while about Jim in her book, but I don't think I was much help. It was a nice day, anyway. We wandered around Sausalito and browsed in the bookstore there. I bought a few teenage romances for myself, and my mother bought a few for herself.

She was exhausted by the time we biked home, and went off to lie down for a while before getting ready for Dad. I climbed out onto my fire escape with one of my teenage romances, *Mean Girl*, and saw the note sticking up in the pot with the withered begonia.

I unrolled it and read:

> *New development. Can you meet me in front of the aquarium on Sunday at 2?*
>
> *J.*

I wrote:

> *Yes!*
>
> *R.*

I spent the rest of the afternoon reading *Mean Girl*. The boy in the story, naturally, was six feet tall, had dark hair and loved animals.

Chapter 8

Jason wasn't there when I arrived at the aquarium. There was the usual assortment of families with parents dragging unwilling kids into the building or kids dragging unwilling parents. I pulled my bike off to the side and sat down on one of the steps.

What had happened, I wondered. I hadn't had a chance to do any serious thinking about Jason yesterday between Karen, my mother and *Mean Girl*. If I weren't meeting Jason today, I'd be home reading *A Kiss for Glenda* or *Too Many Boys*. I began thinking about my own father. What if he just disappeared suddenly, the way Jason's father had disappeared? What if today, for instance, when I arrived home, my mother told me that my father wasn't coming back? I could feel a sick feeling spreading up from my stomach. How could I stand it if my father just suddenly disappeared?

A little old man sat down next to me and began coughing. I moved a little farther away from him and tried to control my thoughts. Calm down, I said to myself. Your father isn't going anywhere, just to Grandpa's store. He'll be back. He always comes back. Maybe he'll be tired and cranky but who cares. Tomorrow he'll be himself again, making up funny poems, eating banana muffins. . . .

The old man kept coughing and coughing. He moved a little closer to me and I moved away. Why couldn't people with colds stay home instead of spreading their lousy germs all over the place? I shot him a dirty look and he smiled at me. Poor man! He had hardly any teeth, and his beard was practically all white. How could you be angry at such an old, sickly man? I looked away quickly. Where was Jason anyway?

But fathers do disappear. Not only the way Jason's father had, but other fathers as well. Melinda Mason's father just walked out one day and she hardly ever sees him anymore. Lots of parents get divorced. I tried to think of what would happen if my parents were divorced. Who would I live with? Would they divide us up—Arthur and me? Oh God! I couldn't stand thinking about my parents splitting up and getting a divorce.

The old man was sneezing now. He moved a little closer, jamming me up against the wall. Then he pulled an American flag out from his pocket and started sneezing into it. He was pressed up as close to me as he possibly could without sitting in my lap.

It was too much. I don't go in for any of that patriotic, flag-waving stuff, but I don't like to see anybody sneezing into the American flag either. Especially when he's obviously some kind of sex pervert.

"Now you better stop it, Mister," I hissed at him, "or I'll, I'll . . ."

The old man stopped sneezing. He laid the American flag down on his lap and smiled. "Vot am I doink?" he asked in a strange foreign accent.

"You know very well what you're doing," I said, and jumped to my feet.

"No, vait a minute, little goil," said the old man, and he put out his hand and grabbed my arm.

"Let me go!" I shouted. "Get your hands off me, you . . . you . . ."

The old man began laughing. He was laughing so hard his few teeth suddenly fell out and his beard began slipping over his mouth.

"Boy are you a sucker!" Jason Furst said. He pulled off the wig and the beard he was wearing, and now he was grinning at me with a whole mouthful of teeth.

"But . . . but . . . why . . . ?" I began.

"Oh," said Jason, "I decided you weren't really getting a very favorable impression of me. I thought you might enjoy a few laughs."

"Laughs!" I shouted at him. "That's your idea of a few laughs—sneezing in the American flag and scaring me. . . ."

But he kept laughing, and what do you do when somebody keeps laughing? Either you get mad or you end up laughing too, which is what I finally did.

"But where did you get the beard and the wig and that toothless mouthpiece?"

"I was Rip Van Winkle in a school play a couple of years ago," Jason said. "It's a good thing I thought of bringing all the stuff up here with me when we moved." Jason's cheeks were still pink from laughing so hard and his eyes were very bright. He patted the wig and the beard, looked at me and started laughing again.

"Well," I said, "it's good to see you laughing. I guess that means things are looking up."

Jason stopped laughing. "No," he said. "They're not."

He folded the wig and beard up carefully and

stowed them away in his daypack. Then he dried off his toothless mouthpiece and put that away too. Neither of us said anything. When he was finished packing everything up, he sighed, fished around in his pocket and pulled something out.

"Here," he said. "This came."

It was a picture postcard from Geneva, Switzerland, showing masses of brilliant flowers banked around a statue of a fawn. The message read:

> *Dear Jason,*
> *You would be astonished at the mottled pinks. The oranges are fine but the reds are shallow and muddy. I miss you very much.*
> *Love,*
> *Dad*

"I've been thinking," Jason said slowly.

I was trying to think too. There was something very strange about the message on that card, something that seemed to say it was a phony and that underneath it was another, real one.

"I've been thinking," Jason continued, "and I'm beginning to believe you may be right."

"Why?" I asked him. I turned the card over and examined the picture carefully.

"My mother," Jason said. "She seemed happy this time when the card came. She couldn't wait to show it to me. Just the opposite of the last card he sent us, when she got hysterical and made us move. This time she smiled and kept saying how great it was that he had a chance to visit Geneva, and that she knew he was having a good time. She kept saying it over and over again about his having a good time. So I began thinking—maybe you're right. Maybe he does work for the CIA. Maybe there's something coded on that card that he was telling her."

I flipped the card over again and studied the message.

"I think," Jason said, "that he's telling her he's safe."

"What do you mean?"

"Well, look at the card. He's telling her that the pinks and reds are no good. He says the orange is fine. Right?"

"Right."

"Well, what does that mean to you?"

"I don't know. What does it mean to you?"

"Pinks and reds—could be the communists, right? But orange—what's orange?"

"I give up."

"Orange is Holland. Remember William of Orange? He was from Holland. Orange denotes Holland, and that's where my father is now. He's safe in Holland. That's what he's telling my mother. I guess they were after him in Paris, but he must have gotten away."

"But Jason," I told him. "This card is from Switzerland. It's got a Swiss postmark."

Jason chuckled. "That's just to throw them off. Obviously, the CIA has a vast network, and my father must have mailed the card to his Swiss connection."

I studied the card.

"Of course it's lousy thinking there are a whole bunch of killers after him, but it's good knowing he's safe. I guess I can live with that. And I want to thank you, Rebecca. You helped me figure it all out."

I was still looking at the card. "I'm afraid there may be another explanation, Jason," I told him.

"What?"

"Well, did you notice who this card is addressed to?"

"I handed it to Jason. He looked at it and then at me.

"It's addressed to you, Jason, and so was the last if I remember."

Jason blinked but remained silent.

"See—he's not writing to your mother. He's writing to you. He's not even saying anything about your mother in the cards. She might not have even seen the cards if you didn't want to show them to her. So you can't say he's sending her a coded message."

Jason shook his head. "So what does it mean then?"

"I'm not absolutely sure but—now I don't want to upset you—but, Jason, is it possible your parents have separated?"

Jason was shaking his head very vigorously now. "No, no, no!" he said. "It's impossible. They're very happy together. They never disagree. Only that one time when my mother put a flowering plum tree against the back fence and my father wanted a crab apple. No, no, no! It's impossible. And besides, why would she run away?"

Poor kid, I thought to myself. He doesn't want to admit that his mother could be so vicious. So I just said carefully, "To keep him from knowing where you are."

"But he's been sending me cards."

"Look at the address, Jason. He's been sending them to your old address. They're not being forwarded either. Probably, each time your mother makes one of those mysterious trips of hers, she's picking up the mail. Maybe he's off in Europe trying to figure out what to do next, but when he comes home, he won't even know where to find you. After his first card, I guess your mother figured he was not coming back to her. That's why she got so upset and left town. But she doesn't want you to be suspicious, so she'll keep showing you the cards he mails you, but he doesn't really know where you are."

Jason's eyes began flooding up with tears. I jumped up and grabbed his hand. "Let's do something, Jason. Let's do something to take your mind off things. Later, when the shock wears off a little, we'll discuss it some more."

"But I got used to the idea of him being in the CIA," he said.

"You'll get used to this too," I told him. "You can get used to anything. Donny Kaplan found out that his sister was really his mother, and he got used to that."

"What do you mean?" Jason said. "How could his sister be his mother?"

"Well, she was sixteen years older but he always thought his grandparents were his parents. But they weren't. His sister, only she wasn't his sister, had gotten pregnant the first date she ever went out on and the guy disappeared. So Donny was born and the grandparents said he was their kid and his real mother was his sister, so . . ."

Jason was so confused by Donny Kaplan's genealogy that he forgot to be upset about his parents. It took a while before he finally understood who was who in Donny's family. I didn't want him blubbering all over me again so I said, "Hey, I have an idea."

"What?"

"Why don't I teach you how to ride a bike?"

"No, thanks," said Jason. "That's one thing I don't want to learn. I don't want to learn how to ride a bike and I don't want to learn how to ski. I'm afraid of falling, so why should I learn to ride a bike or to ski?"

"You can't go through life like that," I told him. "And besides, this is California. Everybody in California rides a bike or skis."

"Not me," said Jason.

"So what do you do," I asked him, "besides kicking rabbits?"

Jason remained silent.

"Do you swim?"

"No."

"Do you jog?"

"No."

"Play tennis?"

"No."

I stood up and tugged at his arm. "Come on, Jason, we're going to make an American out of you."

He put up a little fight but not enough to discourage me. I pulled him out to Kennedy Drive and began Lesson #1.

"You're lucky it's Sunday," I told him, "because this part of the park is closed to traffic on Sundays. Here, hold the handlebars and sit up on the seat."

"Don't let go."

"I'm not going to let go. Just get up there and start pedaling."

"I can't reach the pedals."

"That's because I'm a little taller than you." Actually, I was about half a head taller, but I didn't want to rub it in. "Just stretch a little. Come on, Jason, try!"

"Promise me you won't let go."

"Okay, I promise."

Jason was not the first person I had ever taught to

ride a bike. My father and I taught Arthur when he was five, and I taught Karen Blue all by myself three years ago. But Jason seemed a hopeless case. His hands froze on the handlebars, so he couldn't steer, and his body kept listing to one side or the other. And he never stopped peering over his shoulder to make sure I was holding on. What a klutz he was, and if it weren't for his family problems, I'd never have persevered.

After about an hour of absolutely no progress, we both agreed to end Lesson #1.

"I'm thirsty," Jason said.

"Me too," I agreed, wiping the sweat off my forehead.

"It really is very nice of you to take all this trouble teaching me," Jason said formally. "I'd like to treat you to something. What would you like?"

"We could have tea in the Japanese Tea Garden," I told him. "It costs twenty-five cents for kids to get in, but the tea drinking is fun and not very expensive. And there are lots of pretty plants."

"Let's go," said Jason. "My treat."

"No it's not your treat," I told him. "I don't approve of boys paying for girls. I can pay for myself."

"It has nothing to do with my being a boy and your being a girl," Jason insisted. "I just want to show my appreciation because you really earned it, pushing me on that bike."

"I offered to teach you."

"No, no, no!" Jason said. "I insist."

We walked my bike over to the tea garden and I chained it up outside while we continued arguing. He was so eager to treat me that finally I said okay. Jason began fishing around in his pocket for money.

"One small problem," he said finally, grinning at me.

"Let me guess," I told him. "You don't have any money."

"I do," he said. "I have thirty cents, so if you could just lend me—let's see—"

"Don't forget, you have to leave a tip."

"Oh—I was forgetting the tip. It's a good thing you reminded me. So, let's see—"

"And how are you getting home?"

"That's right. That's right. Add my bus fare— Hmm— Better make it a dollar and a half. It's easier to remember that way."

"And you already owe me forty cents."

"I know and I meant to bring it but I forgot."

"You said you'd put it in the begonia plant."

"I will, Rebecca. I swear I will. Look for it tonight."

"Okay! Then with the dollar fifty, you'll owe me a dollar ninety."

"Why don't you give me a dollar sixty so with the forty cents it will come to an even two bucks?"

I fished in my pocket.

"Guess what?" I told him.

"I know," he said. "You don't have any money either."

We unlocked my bike and walked over to the drinking fountain behind the concert pavilion. Jason and I took turns drinking deep swigs of water. Then we sat on the grass and Jason asked me a whole lot of questions about my family, my friends and the things I like to do. He even listened to my answers.

"Do you ever go anyplace without that bike?" he asked as we finally got up to go home.

"Sure I do."

"Next time why don't you leave it home?"

"What next time?"

"Tomorrow afternoon. Let's have tea in the tea garden."

"I can't tomorrow afternoon. I have to do the laundry."

"Well," said Jason, "I'm not sure about Tuesday. I'd better leave you a note in the begonia plant."

"And don't forget my forty cents."

Jason's dark eyes opened wide. "You can count on me," he said.

Chapter 9

I didn't see Jason the next day but I did bump into his mother, and I do mean bump. She was coming out of the elevator, carrying two large bundles, and I was going in with my laundry. She was moving pretty fast, and after we bumped, one of her bundles broke.

Maybe I should have looked where I was going, as she pointed out in a loud, shrieky voice while I helped her pick up three cans of boneless and skinless sardines, a package of English muffins, a head of lettuce, two Bermuda onions (she said there were three, but I couldn't find the third) and another box of that cheap detergent Jason managed to spill a week ago. On the other hand, she could have looked where she was going too, and she certainly could have thanked me for helping her pick up her groceries.

But she didn't. She jerked her head curtly in my direction and said in a tight, icy voice, "You had better look where you're going next time!"

She didn't look at all like Jason, I thought as I worked my laundry over. She was dark and hard featured with a sharp chin and veins that stood out in her neck. Just the kind of woman, I decided, who would kidnap a kid, hide him away from his own father and abuse him. Jason and I hadn't really discussed his mother, I reflected as I pinned back the sleeves of Arthur's SAN FRANCISCO GIANTS sweat shirt and punched it into shape. How to get word to his father where he really was. I didn't want to upset Jason—yesterday there had been some fun moments and it was good to see him happy—but, as I snapped one of my mother's bras in the air, I decided that the next time I saw Jason, we would have to work out a plan.

"Really," said my father that night as he dished out some curried eggplant and stewed cucumbers, "I think I'm going to like our new neighbors very much."

"Oh?" said my mother. "But we never see them."

"That's what I mean," said my father. "The woman seems very nice."

"I didn't know you'd spoken to her."

"I haven't," said my father. "I've only seen her twice, and each time she averted her eyes. I used to be afraid to stick my nose outside because the Hendersons always seemed to be there, waiting to talk to me. But this woman appears to be a very pleasant, quiet, private kind of person."

"I think she's mean," I said.

"Rebecca is friendly with her son," my mother said carefully.

"He seems a very nice boy too," said my father, passing around some warm hard-boiled eggs.

"I don't like warm hard-boiled eggs," said Arthur.

"I don't like them either," said my father, "but I forgot to make them until an hour ago."

"You could invite your friend over one day," my mother said to me.

"I never hear a peep out of him," said my father. "I was afraid he would play the piano all the time, but he never does."

"Maybe his mother is the one who plays the piano," said Arthur.

"Well, I never hear her either. They really seem to be lovely people and outstanding neighbors."

"Why did you say she was mean?" asked my mother, trying to look cool. I recognized the look and realized that I had been careless.

"Uh—well—I just don't think she's—ah—very friendly."

"Has the boy—Jason—that's his name, isn't it, dear? Has Jason said anything about her?"

"No," I said truthfully, "he hasn't. And this curried eggplant is really delicious, Dad. Maybe I'll have a little more."

I avoided my mother's eyes, and we spent the rest of dinner listening to all the reasons why Arthur hated warm hard-boiled eggs and a few others from my father. Neither of them ate any.

Later, when I checked the begonia, I found a note which read:

> *Must stay home tomorrow to wait for the phone company. Can we meet on the fire escape at 4? My mother will be away.*
>
> *J.*

I wrote:

> *Okay!*
> *R.*

Both of my parents were home the next afternoon. They were in the kitchen, drinking coffee and arguing. Tuesday is usually a good day for fighting in my family.

Weekends are off limits because my father is working and Mondays he needs to recuperate.

"You're the one," grumbled my father, "who wanted to go to Death Valley over Christmas. I told you I wanted to stay home."

"Uh uh," shouted my mother, her eyes flashing. "You were the one who said you were tired of cities, tired of the noise, the foul air! You were the one quoting Thoreau all over the place."

"There you go again," said my father, clenching his teeth, "misinterpreting everything I say. I never said I wanted to go to Death Valley. Why should I go to Death Valley? Why should anybody go to Death Valley?"

"Ha!" said my mother. "You can say that to me when only last month you wrote three poems—three pretty feeble poems too, but as usual I didn't say anything—all about finding life in Death Valley, and you said to me that you needed to go to a desert because—"

"I did not."

"Look, kids," I said, "I don't want to interrupt or anything but I'm home, and I have to study for a big test so I'm going out onto the fire escape and I'll be busy there all afternoon."

"Fine, fine!" said my mother, waving at me. My father smiled quickly and then the two of them resumed hostilities. I grabbed a few of my grandmother's chocolate-ripple cookies and headed for the fire escape. It was only three forty-five, so I had to wait fifteen minutes before Jason opened his window and joined me.

"Too bad we couldn't have tea in the Japanese Tea

Garden today, but I have to wait for the phone installer."

"Don't you already have a phone?" I asked. "You've been here a few weeks, and usually the phone company isn't that slow."

"We do have a phone," Jason said, "but now my mother wants another one—in her room."

"Why is that?"

"I don't know." Jason shrugged his shoulders. I was about to ask him a few more questions about why his mother needed another phone, when he noticed the cookies I had stacked off on one side. "What are those?"

"My grandmother's chocolate-ripple cookies. Here, have a few."

"Thanks," Jason said. "Why don't we go into my house and have some milk to go with them?"

"Are you sure it's okay?" I said. "I mean, what about your mother?"

"She won't be back until after five."

"Are you sure?"

He nodded grimly. "She goes to a psychiatrist now. Every Tuesday afternoon from four to five."

He didn't have to urge me. I was eager to have a look around Jason's house.

"Watch the plants," Jason said as we climbed over the windowsill.

It's a strange feeling standing inside a room that you've known for years and suddenly it's no longer the same. When the Hendersons lived next door, the room I was now standing in belonged to their son Peter. Even though he had grown up, the room had remained about grade six. Model airplanes had hung from the ceiling, football banners draped the walls, and shelves full of boys' games stood against the walls. The room had been painted blue, and there was a blue carpet on the floor, a red, white and blue spread on the bed and a matching pair of drapes at the window.

Now the room was painted white, the floor was bare, there were no drapes at the window and no furniture except for two long narrow tables holding up pots and pots of African violets. There were pink ones, white ones and more shades of purple than I had ever believed possible.

"It's awesome!" I told Jason. "I never saw so many African violets in my whole life. And they're all blooming!"

"Oh," he said carelessly, "you should have seen the ones we had in Santa Monica."

"But they're all so beautiful—and so healthy. Don't any of them ever get sick? Don't any of them ever die?"

"We lost a few on our way up here, but my mother had cuttings so it wasn't too bad. Come on, I'll show you the rest of the house."

We wandered through the rooms and I was surprised. I guess I was expecting a dismal, dungeonlike decor, but the apartment was furnished in a warm, comfortable style. There were soft chairs in the living room in gold and orange colors, bright paintings on the walls and Persian carpets on the floor. Naturally, plants stood, hung and nestled all over the place, but there still were spaces in between for humans.

Jason's bedroom didn't have model planes or football banners, but except for the plants, it was clearly identifiable as a kid's room—messy with papers, books and clothes thrown all over the place.

"I never thought your mother would let you mess up a room like this," I said.

Jason shook his head. "She's not a nag," he said. "She's always respected my privacy. Maybe something's snapped in her all of a sudden, but you've got the wrong impression, Rebecca."

I followed him into his kitchen—lush, healthy plants hung in baskets from the ceiling and colorful Mexican dishes decorated the walls. We sat down at a redwood table and he poured us some milk.

"Well, you really seemed afraid of her that day down in the basement. And why does she need her own private phone? What is she trying to hide from you?"

Jason was looking at me with surprise. "I have to tell you something, Rebecca."

"She doesn't want you to know where your father is, that's for sure. And she certainly doesn't want him to know where you are."

"I don't know how I can break this to you," Jason said. "You've been such a good friend, and you're smart too. The way you figured out that my parents were separated—I really did admire that."

"It's all right, Jason," I told him. "I only want to help you find your father again. He has to know where you are. She can't keep you apart. Don't worry—we'll find a way."

Jason reached over and patted my hand. "Don't feel bad, Rebecca, but they're not separated. And I'm sorry to tell you this, but I've never been afraid of my mother in my whole life. I've been—I *am* upset because I know something is wrong, but she's a wonderful mother and I'm positive that she and my father are not getting a divorce."

He was looking at me in a worried way, as if I were the one who needed comfort.

"But how do you know? Did you ask her?"

"I don't have to," he said.

"Why not?"

"Now don't feel bad, Rebecca. I knew you were going to be disappointed, and I wouldn't want you to think I don't value your opinion."

"Okay, Jason, just tell me why. How do you know they aren't getting a divorce?"

"Because of the piano," he said.

"The piano?"

"That's right. I figured it out as soon as I got home on Sunday. You see, if they were separated, she never would have taken the piano."

"Why not?"

"Because," he said patiently, "because he's the only one who plays it. She got rid of everything she said we wouldn't be needing. If he weren't coming back, she would have gotten rid of the piano too."

His logic was indisputable. "Yes," I agreed. "You're obviously right."

Jason sighed. "I'm glad you're taking it so well."

"Listen, Jason," I told him. "You've got a mistaken impression of me too. I'm not so self-centered that I can't be wrong once in a while. I'm glad your parents aren't getting a divorce. And I'm glad your mother isn't abusing you, but then, that means . . ."

"I know," Jason said sadly. "I know. I mean I don't know."

"He could be in the CIA," I said, trying to sound enthusiastic.

Jason shook his head. "No," he said, "but it was fun pretending."

Now I patted his hand. "Don't worry, Jason, we'll figure it out."

"I hope so," he said.

Then he smiled at me. "You've got a lot of freckles," he said.

"I know."

"You've got more freckles than anybody I know."

"Thanks a lot."

"I never saw a face with so many freckles. I wonder how many you've got. Must be thousands."

"Look, Jason," I said. "Why don't we change the topic of conversation? What do you think of sea gulls?"

"I bet you could win a contest."

"Cut it out, Jason. Enough is enough."

"But it's lovely. With your soft skin and pink cheeks, your face looks like the heart of a Nomocharis lily."

"A what?"

"A Nomocharis lily—a rare and beautiful plant, very hard to cultivate. It comes from the high mountains where western China, north Burma and southeast Tibet meet, where the headwaters of the Irrawaddy, Salween, Mekong and Yangtze rivers are each separated by high mountain divides."

That was when I suddenly could hear my heart beating inside my ears. No boy had ever said my face looked like anything, much less the heart of a flower.

Jason was talking about Nomocharis lilies now, and I

was pretending to listen. But I wasn't hearing what he was saying. I was looking at his smooth face with its large, dark, sad eyes and his fair, curly hair, and I wasn't thinking about anything. I was just sitting in Jason's kitchen, looking at his face and not hearing what he was telling me about Nomocharis lilies.

But there were other sounds I couldn't help hearing. A loud crashing sound and then a voice screaming.

"My God!" said Jason. "What's that?"

It was coming from outside.

Two voices yelling. What were they saying? "Rebecca! Rebecca! Rebecca!"

"It's me," I told Jason. "They're calling me."

I hurried into the room with the African violets and threw open the window. My mother was crawling around on the fire escape shouting, "Rebecca!" and I could hear my father's voice from up on the roof also yelling, "Rebecca!"

"What's going on?" I said.

"Oh, thank God, thank God!" said my mother. My father, from up on the roof, continued to shout, "Rebecca!"

"It's all right, Michael," she screamed. "She's safe. She's all right."

"Of course I'm all right," I said. "What did you think happened to me?"

"I couldn't imagine," said my mother. "There was a call for you, and when I came in to tell you, you weren't here. Daddy thought maybe you were on the roof but you weren't. And then one of the pots fell off the fire escape, and I didn't want to look down because—oh, Rebecca darling, what happened?"

My father came hurrying down the ladder from the roof. "Rebecca, Rebecca, what happened?" he asked.

Jason was standing next to me. There were African violets all around us—the pinks on my side, the whites on his, and the purples and violets everywhere else.

"Uh . . . Mom, Dad," I said, "this is my friend Jason Furst."

Chapter 10

The pot that had fallen off the fire escape contained the dying begonia. Jason went downstairs to examine the remains.

"The poor thing has gone to its maker," he reported. "May it rest in peace. And while we're on that subject, Rebecca, why not administer final rites to all the other terminal patients as well?"

He quickly gathered up the other dead or dying plants and carried them off my fire escape.

"I don't know," I told him when he returned. "It looks so empty now. I guess I'm used to them."

Jason shuddered.

"And then it was fun leaving notes for each other."

"But that was only because I didn't want my mother to know we were friends. She seemed to have a . . . ah . . . mistaken impression of you. But I know she'll change her mind once she meets you."

"I'm not so sure—especially if she ever finds out what I thought of her."

"She won't." Jason looked at his watch. "She'll be home soon, and I think I'll introduce you formally to her today."

We were sitting out on the fire escape again. It felt very lonely without my sick plants.

"There is another reason I liked leaving messages in the begonia," I told Jason.

"What is it?"

"Well, my mother is a writer—I told you that. But what I didn't tell you is that she always manages to put me into her books."

"Say, that's neat," Jason said. "Do you think she'd want to put me in a book?"

"I'm sure she would," I told him, "and that's just the problem. I don't have any privacy because she manages to put everything I do or say into her books one way or another."

Jason was looking at me, puzzled.

"That's why I hardly ever talk on the telephone, because she's always listening in."

"But what do you say that you don't want her to repeat?"

"It isn't that. It's just that she takes everything I do and makes it better than it really is in my own life."

"Like what?"

"Well—like all the girls in her stories do great things. They become ballerinas or they get beautiful dollhouses. Nothing that special ever happens to me."

"What is she working on right now?"

I could feel the heat rising up behind my eyeballs. He was looking at me out of a face fresh with innocence. How could I tell him my mother was writing a romance? What did Jason Furst know about romance? A lot less than I, that was for sure. He had been so busy potting his begonias, I wondered if he knew the difference between girls and boys. My luck! All the boys in the teenage novels I read were always more experienced than the girls. Why did I have to fall for a skinny, little crybaby who couldn't even ride a bike?

Because he said my face was like the heart of a lily, that was why. Because of one careless sentence, I was already changing my mind about bunnies. What power there lay in words!

"So what's she doing now?" Jason asked again.

"Uh—listen, Jason, did I hear your mother?"

I didn't, but about fifteen minutes later she stuck her head out of the window. Jason performed the introductions. Mrs. Furst did not appear enthusiastic, but she was polite.

My mother was much more enthusiastic. She seemed to credit Jason with saving my life.

"A very nice boy," my mother said, looking hopefully at me.

"He's interested in flowers," I said calmly. She looked away, disappointed. "And how's the book going, Mom?"

"Not bad, not bad! I'm nearly finished with the first draft, and I'll be interested to see what you think."

After dinner, my mother began looking for her purse. At least once or twice daily she misplaces it, and sometimes the whole family has to form itself into a search party before it's found again. But my father was taking a shower, and Arthur was ankle-deep in his baseball cards. So I fell in with her as we explored all the possible places it could be hiding.

"Michael!" yelled my mother, banging on the bathroom door. "Is my purse in there?"

"What?" yelled my father, inside the shower.

"Never mind, Michael."

"What?"

"I said never mind."

"Never mind what?"

"Never mind."

I finally found my mother's purse on top of the refrigerator. She carried it into her bedroom and I followed her.

"Mom," I said, "tell me again how you fell in love with Dad."

"Oh, honey, you've heard that story so many times."

"Just once more, Mom."

"Okay, well you know I met him in his father's store and he told me how to treat a sty. When I went back to thank him, he asked me to go out to a movie. Well, I had a bad cold but I went anyway, and he wrote a poem and mailed it to me."

"What kind of a poem?"

My mother giggled like a young girl. "That's why I fell in love with him."

"Because he wrote the poem?"

"Uh huh."

"Say it, Mom, say it."

"You've heard it so many times, Rebecca, but, okay, the poem went like this:

> I think that I shall never see
> A nose like yours that runs so free.
> A nose whose red and bruised tip
> Hangs droopily above a swollen lip.

"He certainly has written lots of poems about you since," I said.

"Yes," my mother agreed, "beautiful ones too, but that first one is my favorite."

It made me happy thinking how my mother fell in love with my father because he had written a poem. I wanted to tell her that I had fallen in love too because

Jason said my face was like a flower. If she was just my mother and not a writer as well, I would have told her.

She didn't notice me looking hungrily at her. She was smiling to herself, deep in some good, happy memory.

My father, in his frayed terry bathrobe, his hair wispy wet, came into the bedroom. "What were you banging on the bathroom door for?" he demanded. "Why can't I ever take a shower without somebody banging on the door?"

"I was looking for my purse," said my mother, smiling at him.

My father snorted. "Looking for your purse!" But he caught her smile, and he shook his head at her and then the two of them burst out laughing.

I was glad my parents were in love. And I was glad too that, wherever he was and whatever had happened to him, Jason's father was not separated from his mother.

"How come I still haven't met him?" Karen Blue wanted to know. She was talking about Jason. It was Friday night and she was sleeping over at my house.

"Because his mother went away today. I told you she goes away every week for a night or two, and when she does, he has to sleep over at his mother's friend's house."

"Well, why don't you point him out to me at school?"

"He doesn't go to our school."

"Why not?"

"He goes to private school. He's very smart and his mother wants him to have a classical education."

"You mean with Latin and Greek?"

"Uh huh."

"Yuk! He sounds like a snob."

"I guess he is," I agreed.

"Well, how come you picked him for a boyfriend?"

"Look, Karen," I told her carefully, "I keep telling you he's not my boyfriend. He's just a good friend. I never met anybody like him before. He's very interesting. He knows all about trees and plants and . . ."

Karen wasn't listening. "I have to make a call," she said. "I told Timmy I wasn't sure when we'd be finished with dinner, so I'd better call him. You can tell your mother I don't mind if she listens."

When she came back, Karen said, "Timmy and I are going roller-skating on Sunday. How about you and your—I mean, Jason—how about you two meeting us in the park?"

"No!" I said quickly. "No!"

"Why not?"

"Because . . . because . . . I'm not sure he'll be back, and besides, I have other plans."

I couldn't tell her that Jason Furst couldn't even ride a bike, much less roller-skate.

As it was, Jason didn't return for the whole weekend. I sat on my bare, lonely fire escape and thought about him and all the mysterious circumstances leading up to his father's disappearance. So many things began to fall into place, but first I needed to talk to Jason.

I didn't see him Monday because I was busy doing the laundry. But on Tuesday he joined me on the fire escape.

"How was your weekend?" I asked him.

"A real bore," he said, "a wasted weekend. Alice is

really a very nice woman, but she keeps dragging me off to her Succulent Society meetings. Anybody can grow succulents. There's no challenge there."

He looked at me thoughtfully. "Now there's an idea. Maybe your family would be interested in succulents."

"Maybe."

"You say your mother likes ferns." Jason shook his head. "Ferns are temperamental, very susceptible to temperature changes. But succulents—you could even keep succulents out here. It's almost impossible to kill a succulent. But anyway, guess what?"

"What?"

"Another card came."

He held it out to me. It was from Salzburg, Austria, and showed a magnificent rose garden in front of an old castle.

> *Dear Jason,* [*it said*]
> *Gather ye rosebuds while ye may seems particularly true in this setting. But we must also remember that there is no rose without a thorn. Miss you as much as ever.*
> *Love,*
> *Dad*

This card was addressed to the San Francisco address. Jason didn't need to point it out to me. I could see for myself.

"No letters or cards ever come for your mother, do they?" I asked.

"No."

"But she doesn't complain."

"She tries not to," Jason said. "Now that she's been going to a psychiatrist, she must do all her crying and complaining there. When she's with me, she tries to be calm and cheerful. But I can feel her suffering underneath."

"Jason, I've been meaning to ask you," I said, "what's your father's name?"

"Roger—Roger Franklin Furst."

"Do you happen to have a picture of him?"

"Of course," he said softly. "I have one in my wallet." He pulled it out and showed it to me. There were two of them in the picture, smiling, a very good-looking man and a small, skinny boy with the same face and the same smile.

"Why, you look just like him," I said.

Jason didn't say anything, but his breathing suddenly sounded jagged.

"Look, Jason," I said softly, "why don't you just try to believe he's away on a business trip? Why do you have to know where he is? Maybe there's a good reason why your mother doesn't want you to know."

"I don't think so," Jason said. "Either she doesn't trust me or she's trying to protect me. But I need to know the truth."

"Do you want me to help you?"

"Yes," he said. "I do."

"Because," I told him, "I have another idea, but you may not like it. So I want you to be sure."

He didn't look at me but he nodded his head. "I'm sure," he said.

So that's why I did it. Because I think he really knew the truth. But he needed a friend to give him that one little extra push. All of the evidence added up—the phony cards that came only for Jason, his mother's mysterious weekly trips out of town, and now the psychiatrist.

I made the phone call from a pay phone the next afternoon before I came home from school. Then I rang Jason's doorbell. His mother answered the door and tried to smile when she saw me standing there. What would she think of me after I told Jason? Would she ever forgive me?

"Hello, Mrs. Furst," I said nervously. "Is Jason in?"

"Well . . . yes, Rebecca, I think he is."

"May I see him, please?"

She didn't move, but Jason heard me and came quickly to the door. "Hi, Rebecca, come on in."

"No, I don't think so, but how about coming out for a walk with me?"

"Right now?"

"Uh huh. There's something I want to talk to you about."

"I'll get my jacket."

We walked along the street together and he began chattering. He didn't stop. He was telling me about a Greek play his school was planning to perform, using masks the way they did in ancient times. He talked about papier-mâché masks and how simple it would be to make masks, even for somebody like himself.

"Jason," I said, "I made a call today."

"Maybe we could go over to the library and I could see if they have anything I could use."

"I talked to a man and he asked me how old I was."

". . . I probably will have to go down to the main library or use the one over at Berkeley for the actual pictures of the Greek masks."

"When I told him I was fourteen, he wasn't sure he should tell me, but then I reminded him it was public information so he said okay."

"I might even have to talk to some classical authorities."

"Jason, I know where your father is."

He stopped talking and turned a face filled with misery towards me. There were tears welling up in his eyes.

"It's the only place he could be, Jason, and I think you know it too. Those postcards are blinds. And the fact that they only come for you has to mean that your mother is in touch with your father some other way. Maybe that's why she installed her own phone. When she leaves town once a week, she must be seeing him. But why is she so anxious to keep it a secret from you? And why does she need to see a psychiatrist? There's only one possible answer."

Jason was looking over my head. He said absolutely nothing.

"I don't have to tell you where he is if you don't want to hear it."

The tears were running down his face now.

"Just tell me to stop and I will."

"No," Jason said, "I want to know."

"I called the Department of Corrections this afternoon, Jason." I began crying too. Both of us stood there crying and I told him.

"Your father is in jail."

Chapter 11

My mother tried to break it to him gently. She had soft music playing when he got home and waited until he had drunk half a glass of wine before telling him.

"Tonight!" he said. "Tonight!"

"Well, darling," said my mother gently, "I really didn't know how to get out of it."

"Why didn't you just say we were busy?"

"She caught me off guard. She rang the bell and when I opened the door she was standing there with a great big smile on her face. I nearly fell over."

"I thought she had better sense," said my father. "I never thought she was going to turn out like the Hendersons."

"Anyway, darling, she just went on and on about how she had been meaning to have us all over to dinner and how she was making this big cioppino and wanted us to come tonight."

My father groaned.

"It's not so bad, Daddy," I said. "Jason says before his father went to jail his mother used to be a real gourmet cook."

"I don't like fish," Arthur said.

My father brightened. "That's right. Arthur doesn't like fish. I remember he even gets rashes if he eats fish. Maybe I'll take him out for a hamburger tonight, and you two go and have dinner next door."

"It's all right, Dad," Arthur said. "I don't like fish, but I told Mrs. Furst and she said she would make some fried chicken too."

"It's not good manners to tell your hostess you don't like what she's serving," I told Arthur.

"Why not?" said Arthur.

"Because it just isn't."

"She didn't mind," Arthur said. "And besides, I think it's worse manners to invite somebody to your house for dinner and feed him something he doesn't like."

"That's right," said my father, "and especially when they don't give you any notice."

"Now, now, now," said my mother, "you know you like cioppino very much, Michael. We're not going until seven thirty anyway, so why don't you finish your wine and take a nice, hot shower and maybe a little nap?"

My father tried to rally his spirits, and by seven thirty all of us, dressed and smiling, were standing outside Jason's door.

My mother rang the bell. Unlike the first time, we heard quick footsteps and a smiling Mrs. Furst opened the door.

"Come in, come in," she welcomed us.

My mother handed her one of my grandmother's prune cakes.

"This must be one of your grandmother's famous prune cakes, Rebecca. Jason has told me several times how delicious it is. Thank you so much. I can't wait to try it."

We ate our cioppino out of deep colorful Italian

bowls, and Arthur had a big plate of fried chicken all to himself.

"I really was eager to have you all over for dinner," said Mrs. Furst, "because I expect I'm going to be terribly busy after this, and I didn't want you to think I was unfriendly."

My father shook his head vigorously. "We'd never think that, Mrs. Furst."

"Why don't you call me Gladys, Michael?"

"Don't worry, Gladys," said my father, "about our thinking you unfriendly."

"Well, I'm afraid I must have made a terrible first impression," Gladys Furst said, passing around the french bread. "Especially to Rebecca."

"No, no, no!" my father protested.

"That's very kind of you, Michael, but I was so worried about Jason finding out, I guess I must have gone off my head temporarily. Thank goodness he knows now. Everybody knows now, and I don't feel anywhere as ashamed as I thought I would."

"Does he wear a uniform?" Arthur asked.

Mrs. Furst looked puzzled.

"Your husband. Does he have to wear a uniform?"

"Yes he does, but it fits him very well. He's a very well built man, I must say, and all the years he's spent gardening have made him extremely muscular. But anyway, I will be looking for a job starting next week. Actually, I'm looking forward to it. My husband always babied me—and Jason too. He thought we needed to be protected like his hothouse flowers. That's why he always wanted money—for us. Weekends, I guess I'll go down to Chino—that's where my husband is—so I may not have too much time for socializing."

My father poured himself some more wine and smiled a big, happy smile. "We'll understand, Gladys," he said.

"If you like," said my mother, "Jason can stay with us while you're gone."

"That's very nice of you, Catherine, but my friend Alice is very happy to have him stay with her."

"From now on," said Jason, "I'm going to stay by myself."

"But Jason," said Mrs. Furst, "you're only—"

"Fourteen," said Jason, trying to keep his voice deep and manly. "Old enough to look after myself."

"I don't know," said Mrs. Furst, doubtfully.

"Fourteen and a half," Jason added.

"Well," said his mother, wavering, "if you really think you can."

"I really do," said Jason, firmly.

"And of course, it won't be every weekend that you'd have to stay up here. Sometimes you can come down with me and entertain yourself while I go to see Daddy, and, Jason, I do have some good news for you."

"What is it?"

"I didn't want to say anything until I was sure, but the prison does allow family visits. They have special apartments to put up the families of prisoners, and Daddy would be able to stay with us for the whole weekend. Of course, some of the other prisoners want to use the facilities too, so we may not be able to get you in as often as we'd like, but maybe once a month."

Mrs. Furst never stopped talking about her husband and the prison he was in. It was almost as if he had made Harvard.

"Of course we knew he would be sent to a minimum-security prison, but right away everybody could see he was not just an ordinary prisoner. He made a special point of telling the gardener that the soil was all wrong and that the drainage was a serious problem. He's planning to replace all the shrubs on the north side of the prison and also to plant a special succulent garden with many varieities of *Echeveria* as well as *Aeonium, Cotyledon* and *Crassula*. Then, of course, he does plan on having them build a small hothouse just for begonias, and I suppose by the time he's through he'll be giving courses in horticulture. They're certainly lucky to get him, I can tell you. I know for a fact the prison at Tehachapi would give their eyeteeth to have him. From what I hear, they don't even know how to grow Shasta daisies."

"There," said my mother, after we came home, "now that wasn't so bad, was it, Michael?"

"No," my father admitted, "but from what she says, her husband should be out in no time. That parole board will let anybody out, even somebody who—"

"Plays the piano?" I said.

"Well," said my father, "I suppose it could be worse. He could play the drums."

I told my grandmother about Jason's father, and she was concerned at first when she heard. She was restocking the freezer with our weekly supply of cakes and cookies. The two of us were alone in the kitchen.

"Tried to burn down his business?" she said. "What a crazy thing to do."

"It was all because there was going to be a big international begonia show, and he didn't think he could go because he had so much work to do. He just lost his head. He thought if he could burn it down at night when nobody was there, he could collect the insurance and spend the rest of his life with his plants."

"And his son lives next door?"

"Yes, Grandma, but don't worry. He's a very nice boy."

"I'm sure he is, but—"

"And he's smart and funny."

My grandmother sighed. "You like this boy?" she asked in a worried voice.

"We're just friends," I told her.

"I was afraid of that," she said.

"Look, Grandma, I'm not marrying him. He's a very nice boy, and it's not his fault that his father did a dumb thing. Jason, that's his name, knows all about plants too. He's going to be a botanist when he grows up. I told him about your sick palm tree, and he thinks he might be able to figure out what's wrong with it."

"Well," said my grandmother, "just let me ask you one thing."

"What?"

"Does he write poems?"

"No," I told her, "he doesn't."

"All right," said my grandmother, "then I'm willing to meet him."

Jason showed me a letter his father sent him.

> *Dear Jason,* [*it said*]
> *I suppose you would have had to know sooner or later. Your mother tells me that you are taking it very well—better than either she or I did. It seems we owe you an apology. Not only for bringing this shame upon you, but also for thinking you incapable of handling it.*

Now you know the truth about me. I've been a fool. I thought money was more important than anything else. Thank God nobody was hurt. True, I've hurt you, your mother and my own self. If you can forgive me, I'll try to make it up to you.

Your loving,
Father

P.S. I enclose a garden plan for the eastern corner of the prison. Note the placement of tuberous and fibrous begonias. Would you recommend Coccinea or Diswelliana or both?

"I just wrote back," Jason said, "and I told him about you too."

"You didn't tell him I was the one who found out that he was in jail, did you?"

"It's all right, Rebecca," Jason said. "My father appreciates intelligence. He won't mind. And besides, it's a relief to both my parents finding out I'm not some kind of delicate flower who was just going to wither away if I knew the truth."

"I never did ask you," I said. "How did they manage to send those cards from Europe?"

"My father has business contacts there," said Jason. "They sent him the cards, he wrote them to me and sent them back to be mailed. The first went to the old address because my mother moved in such a hurry. She just panicked. It had nothing to do with the card. She thought one of the neighbors would find out and tell me. Once we moved to San Francisco, she felt safe and could pretend to be happy when the second card arrived. Now she and my father realize they should have told me right away."

We were sitting in Golden Gate Park on another bright Sunday before beginning Jason's Bike Riding Lesson #2.

"How long until your father gets out?" I asked him.

"Maybe a year or so."

"And in the meantime?"

"Well, we all think we should make a fresh start up here. My mother is looking for a job in a nursery."

"With babies?"

"No, of course not, dummy—a plant nursery. And maybe I can work part-time too. It won't be so bad. We've got plenty of money from the sale of the house. We'll manage. And when my father gets out of jail, we don't want him to do anything else but work with plants. Maybe we'll buy a nursery and just specialize in begonias. . . . I can always get a scholarship to school or even"—Jason shuddered—"go to public school the way you do."

"I'm glad you're staying, Jason," I told him.

"I am too."

He was grinning at me now, grinning at my freckles. "You really have a lot of freckles," he said.

I could feel the beating in my ears again. Was he going to say it again—that my face was like the heart of a Nomocharis lily? Was he going to say my face was like some other flower? Or fruit? Or even a vegetable?

But no. He was thinking of something else. He began sighing. "Do I have to?" he said.

"Have to what?"

"Do I have to ride a bike?"

"Not if you don't want to. Some people may despise you and call you a sissy, but if you don't mind . . ."

Jason stood up. "Okay, let's get it over with. I suppose you really do have mobility with a bike, and there are quite a few gardens in Marin I'd like to have a look at."

Lesson #2 went even worse than Lesson #1.

"Look ahead," I kept telling him as I held the seat of the bike and ran along, pushing it. "Stop looking back at me and try to concentrate on keeping your body straight."

"Don't let go," he hollered.

"I'm not letting go. Just look ahead."

It was a disaster.

Jason kept jerking his body around, and suddenly the bike lurched sharply to the left. I couldn't hold it and in a second there lay Jason, all tangled up on the ground with the bike on top of him.

"Ouch!" he yelled. "My leg!"

I rushed forward, murmuring comforting sounds. There was a big tear in the left leg of his jeans, and a bloody, scraped knee showed through the hole.

"That's all right, Jason," I said. "It's just a little scratch."

Jason looked up at me with a woeful face. Naturally, his eyes were beginning to tear. What could I do? What is the best way to stop a person from crying?

I kissed him. I knelt down next to him, bent over his bloody knee and kissed him hard right on his mouth. He was the first boy I had ever kissed in my life (not counting Arthur), so I wasn't terribly good at it. Our foreheads bumped and our teeth banged together hard.

When it was over, Jason looked at me thoughtfully.

"Is that what it's supposed to be like?" he said.

"Well, how should I know?" I told him. "This is the first time for me."

"For me too," he said, "and my forehead hurts." He reached up to rub it, but there weren't any more tears in his eyes.

That night, my mother asked me to read the first draft of her new book, *First Love.* I read it from beginning to end while my mother paced nervously outside my room. Melanie and Jim's first kiss was a lot different from Jason's and mine.

> Jim stood near her, and she shivered from the sense of his closeness.
>
> "Melanie," he said, "I've never really met a girl like you."
>
> She didn't know what to say to him. He was the handsomest, most popular boy in the senior class. She had admired him from afar for so long, it was hard to believe that the two of them were standing there together, outside her house, and that this was their third date.
>
> "You know all about Mary Beth. . . ."
>
> "You don't have to explain about her," she murmured.
>
> "And Ellen . . ."
>
> "You were sorry for her. . . ."
>
> "And Barbara . . ."
>
> "She wouldn't let you alone."
>
> "But you're the first girl I've ever really respected."
>
> She looked away and hoped he couldn't see her flaming cheeks.
>
> "When you saved my dog that day, when you ran in front of the Colonel Sander's truck and snatched

her up, I was only grateful to you. But now that I've seen you with your own animals—the way you mended that crack in your turtle's back . . . the way you delivered those kittens . . ."

One arm was around her waist now, and with his other hand, he gently raised her face to his. "Melanie!" he said.

"Jim!" she replied.

Slowly, powerfully, their lips met and the world stood still for their first kiss.

I don't think the world stood still for my first kiss. My lip even swelled up that night from where my teeth banged against Jason's. I cried when I read the description in my mother's book about Melanie and Jim's first kiss, but I laughed out loud when I looked at my swollen lip in the mirror.

Chapter 12

I told my mother what I thought of her book.

"It's wonderful," I said. "I love it."

My mother blinked.

"Congratulations!" I told her. "This is the first time you've written a book and I'm not in it."

"I told you," said my mother, "that you weren't going to be in it."

"Yes, but you say that every time."

"Well, of course you are supersensitive, Rebecca, you have to admit."

"I don't think so," I told her, "but this time, I have absolutely nothing at all in common with Melanie. She's a nice enough girl, fairly bright. I'm happy she becomes an expert at *taekwondo,* and it's great that she's so crazy about animals."

"Well you like animals too," said my mother.

"Not rabbits," I told her.

"But anyway, Rebecca, what about Jim? What do you think of Jim?"

"Marvelous! I don't know anybody like him."

"What did you think of him as a character?"

"Wonderful! He loves animals and he's a great skier and swimmer, and he's strong and brave—just the kind of boy most girls would want for a boyfriend."

My mother was smiling at me now. She had her head cocked to one side, and she stood there, grinning.

"I warn you, Mom."

"It's all right, Rebecca. Can't I even smile?"

"Not that smile. I don't like it. What's your next book going to be about?"

"I don't know yet."

"Not another romance, I hope. Do something else."

"I might," said my mother sweetly. "Maybe a mystery. I never did a mystery. It could be fun."

I knew she was thinking about Jason's father, and I had the feeling that in her next book, there might be a girl named Alexis whose *mother* might suddenly disappear. Perhaps she would turn up in a South American prison or be kidnapped by a crazy terrorist group. Undoubtedly there would be a boy with *pale* eyes and *dark* hair. It would be my story all over again but more exciting, more colorful, more unbelievable.

And suddenly I didn't care. Because the way I was feeling these days, no story in a book could match what was happening to me.

"That's fine," I told my mother. "Good luck to you, and if I can be any help, let me know. But where are you going with that plant?"

My mother was carrying a large, pink African violet.

"I think we need a west window," replied my mother, smiling fondly into the plant's green leaves. "I think we're getting too much sun in my room."

"Oh? Is that what Jason said?"

"Yes, he thinks I should have only succulents in my room. He thinks ferns are just too unreliable and that if I stick to succulents, with maybe a few hardy African violets in west windows, I shouldn't have any trouble."

"I miss them," I said, "all those sick old plants on my fire escape."

"But Jason's given you a couple of jade plants. They look wonderful."

"I don't know," I said. "They're so healthy looking I feel guilty every time I eat a candy bar in front of them."

"Hmm!" said my mother, "that would be a good line for Alexis in my new book. She's going to love plants."

"Be my guest, Mom," I told her.

Jason and I finally had tea together at the Japanese Tea Garden. As usual, we didn't have enough money. I had thought it was twenty-five cents for kids, but I hadn't realized it was twenty-five cents for kids twelve and under.

"No problem," Jason said. "I always get in places for under twelve."

"Well, I can't," I told him.

Jason surveyed me, lingering, as usual, on my freckles.

"Stoop down," he said finally, "pull in your chest and leave the rest to me."

"Two children," he informed the ticket taker.

The man nodded at Jason but shook his head when he saw me.

"How old are you?" he asked me.

"Twelve," Jason replied.

"I'm not talking to you," said the man. "I'm talking to her."

"But I'm her brother," said Jason.

"Oh yeah? Then how old are you?"

"I'm twelve too," said Jason, opening his big, dark, innocent eyes up wide. "We're twins."

The man snorted. A tour bus pulled up in front of the Japanese Tea Garden, and a whole load of tourists piled out and fell into place behind me. I could feel the laughter rolling around inside and was concentrating very hard on keeping my mouth closed so it wouldn't get out.

"Twins?" said the man finally.

"Yes," said Jason. "I know we don't look alike. She takes after my mother, who has freckles and bony knees and elbows. I look more like my grandfather on my father's side, but my grandmother thinks . . ."

"Is this where you buy the tickets?" asked a woman behind me.

"What's holding everything up?" murmured somebody father down the line.

"Do they need to see our passports?"

". . . her brother on her father's side who had curly hair but . . ."

"Okay! Okay!" said the harried ticket taker, "here's a ticket for you and one for your sister. Just stop talking and GO!"

"Hey," said Jason, pointing to a large tree, as soon as we were inside the gate, "will you look at that *Pinus radiata.*"

But I was too busy laughing. "Imagine being your twin!" I said. "And what did you mean telling him about my bony elbows and knees?" I gave him a quick jab with one of my bony elbows and tried to land a kick with one of my bony knees but he was too fast for me.

We had wonderful seats in the teahouse, overlooking the little pond. While we drank our tea and ate our cookies, Jason entertained me by naming all the trees and shrubs he could see from where we sat.

"Look at that *Pinus thunbergiana*—excuse me, Rebecca, I mean that Japanese pine—espaliered on the bamboo trellis. What a place! I'm so glad we came."

We finished our tea and wandered through the gardens. Jason pointed out the dwarf conifers, the large kiaki tree, and crooned over every growing thing down to the smallest weed. We looked at the shiny goldfish in the ponds, skimming underneath the water lilies, and ended up at last underneath the Moon bridge.

"It's called that," Jason said, "because with its reflection, it forms a perfect circle."

"And when you look down, you can see your face in the water. Come on, Jason, let's climb up."

"I don't know," he said doubtfully. "I might fall."

"You won't fall. I'll be right behind you. Go ahead. Just put your feet on those little wooden ridges, and hold on. Go ahead now."

I stayed right behind him and pushed and shoved until he got to the top. He clung to the sides but once he was up he loved it, and we climbed up another six or seven times.

"You know," he told me later, as we sat on the steep steps in front of the temple gate, "I measured myself today and guess what?"

"What?"

"I'm five foot three now."

"Isn't that nice!" I said enthusiastically. I didn't have the heart to tell him I had measured myself yesterday and was now five foot five and a half.

"I'm really in my growth spurt," said Jason. "A kid in my class said he grew four inches last year."

"That's nice."

"So . . . if I grow four inches this year, let's say by next October I'll be five foot seven."

"Hmm."

Jason reached over, very clumsily, and took my hand. His own hand was damp with nervous perspiration.

"So what do you think, Rebecca? Can you wait a whole year?"

"For what?"

"For me to grow four inches."

"Don't be a jerk," I said, hoping my own hand wouldn't start sweating. "It doesn't matter how tall or short you are."

"No kidding?"

"No kidding."

Jason examined my hand. "Look, Rebecca," he said, "you have a small hand, and look at mine." He put our hands together and it was true, his hand was larger than mine.

"I really think," he said, "that I'm going to end up taller than you because my hand is bigger."

"Don't worry about it."

"I'm not worried. I'm just wondering why your hand is sweating so much."

"My hand!" I yelled. "My hand isn't sweating. Your hand is."

"Well, whosever hand it is, let's wipe them both and start all over again."

In between wipes, we held hands, and the afternoon passed very quickly.

Jason called me that evening and when I answered the phone, I could hear my mother in the kitchen, pretending to get herself a cup of coffee.

"Hey, Rebecca, guess what?"

"What?"

"I think my voice is changing."

"No kidding?"

"No kidding. Listen to me and tell me what you think."

"I listened, but it sounded like the same high, squeaky voice to me. "I can't really tell," I told him. "It's hard to hear over the phone."

"Well, I'll see you tomorrow. No, wait a minute. . . . I can't tomorrow. I have to go to a meeting of my Begonia Society. But the next day, let's get together."

"Okay, what do you want to do?"

"Anything, as long as it isn't on a bike."

"You're not giving up, are you?" I asked.

"I'd like to, if you'd let me. I mean there are certain things in life I figure I'll never be able to do. Riding a bike is one of them."

"Not crying is another, I bet."

"I like crying," Jason said.

"I know," I told him, "but anyway, I want to ask you something."

"What?"

"Where can I see a Nomocharis lily?"

"Hey," said Jason, "where did you ever hear about them? Don't tell me you're getting interested in plants, Rebecca."

He had forgotten and I couldn't exactly come right out and remind him.

"Never mind where I found out about them. Where can I see them?"

"Perth, Scotland," Jason said. "My father and I made a special trip one year to see the collection of a famous grower. They're very hard to cultivate but such beautiful flowers—pink and white and all spotted inside like . . . "

I was waiting.

". . . like . . . Rebecca, you know something?"

"No, Jason, tell me."

"It's your face. . . . It's like . . ."

"Go on, Jason, go on!"

". . . like the heart of a Nomocharis lily."

"Jason," I told him, "I'll meet you the day after tomorrow, and I don't mind if you won't learn to ride a bike and if you're a crybaby and if you're half a head shorter than me. You owe me forty cents and probably I'll never get it back. But I like you just the way you are. And whether or not your voice changes, I'm proud to be your friend."

My mother had tears in her eyes when I hung up.

"Why are you crying?" I asked her.

"Uh . . . it must be something in the coffee," she said.

But I knew it wasn't.

MARILYN SACHS is the author of several books, including BEACH TOWELS and CLASS PICTURES, both Avon Flare titles. She says, "It isn't easy being the child of a writer, as I'm sure my own kids would agree. Writers tend to be snoopy. They are forever looking for new material, and what better place to start than at home?

"So—FOURTEEN is first of all an apology to my children for having invaded their privacy in the past (and a warning that I'm likely to do it again in the future). It's also a mystery—my first, but I hope not my last. And finally, it's a romance between two very unlikely people—who happen to be fourteen."

Mrs. Sachs lives in San Francisco.